Ocean Sea

Alessandro Baricco was born in Turin in 1958. He is the author of six novels, including *Silk* and *Without Blood*, all of which have been translated into English. His latest novel, *Questa Storia*, was recently published to great acclaim in Italy, and he has also produced five collections of essays and a theatrical monologue.

OTHER NOVELS BY ALESSANDRO BARICCO

Silk

Without Blood

An Iliad

Lands of Glass

City

Ocean Sea

Alessandro Baricco

Translated from the Italian by Alastair McEwen

CANONGATE

Edinburgh · London

First published in Great Britain in 2008 by
Canongate Books Ltd, 14 High Street,
Edinburgh, EH1 1TE

First published in the US in 1999 by Alfred A. Knopf,
a division of Random House Inc., New York,
and in Canada by Random House of Canada Limited, Toronto

Originally published in Italy as *Oceano Mare* by Rizzoli Libri, S.p.A., Milan, in 1993

Translation into English by Alastair McEwen

The moral rights of the author and translator have been asserted

Istituto
Italiano
di
Cultura

EDIMBURGO

This English translation was supported by
the Italian Cultural Institute in Edinburgh

British Library Cataloguing-in-Publication Data
A catalogue record for this book is available on
request from the British Library

ISBN 978 1 84767 074 8

Printed and bound in Great Britain
by Clays Ltd, St Ives plc

www.canongate.tv

To Molli,

amata amica mia

BOOK I

~

The Almayer Inn

S AND AS FAR AS the eye can see, between the last hills and the sea—*the sea*—in the cold air of an afternoon almost past, and blessed by the wind that always blows from the north.

The beach. And the sea.

It could be perfection—an image for divine eyes—a world that happens, that is all, the mute existence of land and water, a work perfectly accomplished, truth—*truth*—but once again it is the redeeming grain of a man that jams the mechanism of that paradise, a trifle capable on its own of suspending all that great apparatus of inexorable truth, a mere nothing, but one planted in the sand, an imperceptible tear in the surface of that sacred icon, a minuscule exception come to rest on the perfection of that boundless beach. From afar he would be no more than a black dot: amid nothingness, the nothing of a man and a painter's easel.

The easel is anchored by slender cords to four stones placed on the sand. It sways imperceptibly in the wind that always blows from the north. The man is wearing waders and a large fisherman's jacket. He is standing, facing the sea, twirling a slim paintbrush between his fingers. On the easel, a canvas.

He is like a sentinel—this you *must* realize—standing there to defend that part of the world from the silent invasion of perfection, a small crack that fragments that spectacular stage set of being. As it is always like this, you need only the glimmer of a man to wound the repose of that which would otherwise be a split second away from becoming *truth*, but instead immediately becomes suspense and doubt once more, because of the simple and infinite power of that man, who is a slit, a chink, a small doorway through which return a flood of stories and the enormous inventory of what *could be*, an infinite gash, a marvelous wound, a path made of thousands of steps where nothing can be true anymore but everything *will be*—just as the steps *are* of that woman who, wrapped up in a purple cloak, her head covered, is pacing the beach with measured tread, skirting the backwash of the sea, her feet tracing furrows from right to left across what is by then the lost perfection of the great picture, consuming the distance that separates her from the man until she comes to within a few paces of him, and then right beside him, where it takes nothing to pause and silently look on.

The man does not even turn. He continues staring out at the sea. Silence. From time to time he dips the brush in a copper cup and makes a few light strokes on the canvas. In their wake the bristles of the brush leave a shadow of the palest obscurity that the wind immediately dries, bringing the pristine white back to the surface. Water. In the copper cup there is only water. And on the canvas, nothing. Nothing that may be *seen*.

The north wind blows as it always does, and the woman pulls her purple cloak closer around her.

"Plasson, you have been working for days and days down here. Why do you carry all those colors around with you if you do not have the courage to use them?"

This seems to wake him up. This hits home. He turns to observe the woman's face. And when he speaks, it is not to reply.

"Please, do not move," he says.

Then he brings the brush up to the woman's face, hesitates a moment, rests it on her lips, and slowly runs it from one corner of her mouth to the other. The bristles come away tinged with carmine. He looks at them, dips them ever so slightly in the water, and looks up once more toward the sea. On the woman's lips there lingers the hint of a taste that obliges her to think "sea water, this man is painting the sea with the sea"— and it is a thought that brings a shiver.

For some time now she has already turned around, and is already pacing measuredly back along the immense beach, her steps a mathematical rosary, when the wind brushes the canvas to dry a puff of rosy light, left to float unadorned amid the white. You could stay for hours looking at that sea, and that sky, and everything, but you would find nothing of that color. Nothing that may be *seen*.

The tide, in those parts, comes in before night falls. Just before. The water surrounds the man and his easel, it clutches them, slowly but with precision, they stay there, the one and the other, impassable, like a miniature island, or a wreck with two heads.

Plasson, the painter.

Every evening a boat comes to pick him up, just before sunset, when the water has already reached his heart. This is the way he wants it. He boards the boat, stows away the easel and all, and allows himself to be taken home.

The sentinel goes away. His duty done. Danger averted. Against the sunset the icon that has again failed to become sacred fades away. All because of that manikin and his paintbrushes. And now that he has gone, time has run out. The dark suspends everything. There is nothing that can, in the dark, become *true*.

ONLY SELDOM, and in a way that some people, in those moments, when they saw her, were heard to whisper . . .

"She'll die of it"

or

"She'll die of it"

or perhaps

"She'll die of it"

or even

"She'll die of it."

All around, hills.

My land, thought Baron Carewall.

. . .

IT IS NOT EXACTLY an illness, it could be one, but it is something less, if it has a name it must be lighter than air, say it and it's already gone.

"When she was a little girl, one day a beggar came and began to sing a lullaby, the lullaby startled a blackbird that flew off . . ."

". . . startled a dove that flew off and the fluttering of wings . . ."

". . . the wings that fluttered, the faintest sound . . ."

". . . it must have been ten years ago . . ."

". . . the dove flashed past the window, in a trice, so, and she looked up from her toys and I don't know, a dread came upon her, but it was a blank dread, I mean to say that she was not like one afraid, she was like one on the point of disappearing . . ."

". . . the fluttering of wings . . ."

". . . one whose soul was fleeing . . ."

". . . do you believe me?"

They believed that she would grow and everything would pass. But in the meantime all over the castle they were laying carpets because, it is obvious, she was afraid of her own foot-steps, white carpets, everywhere, a color that could do no harm, soundless footsteps and sightless colors. In the park, the paths were circular with the single bold exception of a pair of snaking avenues that curled to form smooth regular curves—psalms—and this was more reasonable, in fact all you need is a little sensitivity to understand that any blind corner is a possible ambush, and two roads that cross are a perfect geometrical violence, enough to frighten anyone who possesses real sensitivity and all the more so her, who was not exactly possessed *of* a sensitive spirit but, to put it in exact terms, possessed *by* an uncontrollable sensitivity of spirit forever exploded in who knows which moment of her secret life—the merest scrap of a life, young as she was—only to return by mysterious ways to her heart, and her eyes, and hands and all over, like an illness, although it was not an illness, but something less, if it has a name it must be lighter than air, say it and it's already gone.

This is why, in the park, the paths were circular.

Nor should you forget the story of Edel Trut, whose skill in weaving silk was unrivaled throughout the land and that was why he was summoned by the Baron, one winter's day, when the snow lay as tall as children, as cold as the devil, and getting that far was hellish hard, the horse steaming, its hooves slithering about haphazardly in the snow, and the sleigh behind drifting to the leeward, if I don't get there in ten minutes perhaps I'll die, as sure as my name's Edel, I'll die, and what's more without even knowing what the devil the Baron wants to show me that's so important . . .

"What do you see, Edel?"

In his daughter's room, the Baron stands in front of the long wall without windows, speaking softly, with the courtesy of olden times.

"What do you see?"

Cloth of Burgundy, quality stuff, and a landscape like any other, a job well done.

"It is not just any landscape, Edel. Or at least not for my daughter."

His daughter.

It is a kind of mystery, but you must try to understand, using your imagination, and forgetting what is known so that the fancy may roam free, running far off deep within things until it can see how the soul is not always a diamond but sometimes a silken veil—this I can understand—imagine a diaphanous silken veil, anything could tear it, even a glance, and think of the hand that takes it—a woman's hand—yes— it moves slowly and clasps the veil between the fingers, but clasping is already too much, the hand lifts it as if it were not a hand but a puff of wind and enfolds it between the fingers as if they were not fingers but . . . . as if they were not fingers but thoughts. So. This room is that hand, and my daughter is a silken veil.

Yes, I have understood.

"I do not want waterfalls, Edel, but the peace of a lake, I do not want oaks but birches, and those mountains in the background must become hills, and the day a sunset, the wind a breeze, the cities towns, the castles gardens. And if there really must be falcons, at least let them fly, and far away."

Yes, I have understood. There's only one thing: and the men?

The Baron fell silent. He observed all the characters of the enormous tapestry, one by one, as if listening to their opinion. He moved from one wall to the other, but no one spoke. It was to be expected.

"Edel, is there a way to make men who do no evil?"

God Himself must have wondered about that, at the time.

"I know not. But I shall try."

In Edel Trut's workshop they labored for months with the miles of silk yarn that the Baron sent. They worked in silence because, as Edel said, the silence had to be woven into the fabric of the cloth. It was yarn like any other, only you could not see it, but it was there. And so they worked in silence.

Months.

Then one day a cart arrived at the Baron's castle, and on the cart was Edel's masterpiece. Three enormous rolls of cloth as heavy as the crosses borne in processions. They carried them up a flight of stairs and then along the corridors and through door after door until they reached the heart of the castle and the room that awaited them. Just before they unrolled them, the Baron murmured, "And the men?"

Edel smiled.

"And if there really must be men, at least let them fly, and far away."

The Baron chose the light of the sunset to take his daughter by the hand and lead her to her new room. Edel says that she came in and instantly flushed, for wonder, and for a moment the Baron feared that the surprise might be too much, but it was only a moment, because instantly you could hear the irresistible silence of that silken world where lay a fair and most pleasant land and little men suspended in the air, paced with measured tread across the pale blue of the sky.

Edel says—and this he will never forget—that she gazed around for a long moment and then, turning, she *smiled*.

Her name was Elisewin.

She had a most beautiful voice—velvet—and when she walked it was as if she slipped through the air, so that you could not take your eyes off her. Every now and again, for no reason, she liked to run along the corridors, toward who knows what, on those awful white carpets, she stopped being the shadow she was and ran, but only seldom, and in a way that some people, in those moments, when they saw her, were heard to whisper . . .

CHAPTER 3

Y OU COULD GET to the Almayer Inn on foot, by
the path that led down from St. Amand's chapel, but
also by coach, along the Quartel road, or by the
ferryboat that plied the river. Professor Bartleboom arrived by
chance.

"Is this the Peace Inn?"

"No."

"The St. Amand Inn?"

"No."

"The Post Hotel?"

"No."

"The Royal Herring?"

"No."

"Good. Do you have a room?"

"Yes."

"I'll take it."

The register with the guests' signatures lay open on a wooden bookrest. A freshly made bed of paper that awaited the dreams of other people's names. The Professor's pen slipped voluptuously between the sheets.

Ismael Adelante Ismael Prof. Bartleboom

With flourishes and everything. A nice job.

"The first Ismael was my father, the second my grandfather."

"And that one?"

"Adelante?"

"No, not that one there . . . this one."

"Prof.?"

"Mmm . . ."

"It's Professor, isn't it? It means *Professor*."

"What a silly name."

"It's not a name . . . I *am* a Professor, I teach, do you see? I walk through the streets and people say, 'Good morning, Professor Bartleboom,' 'Good evening, Professor Bartleboom,' but it's not a name, it's what I do, I teach . . ."

"It's not a name."

"No."

"All right. My name is Dira."

"Dira."

"Yes. I walk through the streets and people say, 'Good morning, Dira,' 'Good night, Dira,' 'You're looking pretty today, Dira,' 'What a nice dress you're wearing, Dira,' 'You haven't seen Bartleboom by any chance, have you?' 'No, he's in his room, first floor, the last one at the end of the corridor, these are your towels, take them, there's a view of the sea, I hope it won't disturb you.' "

Professor Bartleboom—from that moment on, simply Bartleboom—took the towels.

"Miss Dira . . ."

"Yes?"

"May I be permitted a question?"

"Such as?"

"How old are you?"

"Ten."

"Oh, I see."

Bartleboom—the freshly demoted ex-Professor Bartleboom—took his suitcases and headed toward the stairs.

"Bartleboom . . ."

"Yes?"

"One doesn't ask young ladies their age."

"That's true, excuse me."

"First floor. The last room at the end of the corridor."

IN THE ROOM at the end of the corridor (first floor) were a bed, a wardrobe, two seats, a stove, a little writing desk, a carpet (blue), two identical pictures, a sink with a mirror, a chest, and a little boy: seated on the windowsill (window open), with his back to the room and his legs dangling out into space.

Bartleboom produced a carefully calibrated little cough, so, just to make any kind of noise.

Nothing.

He entered the room, put down his suitcases, walked over to get a closer look at the pictures (identical, incredible), sat down on the bed, took off his shoes with evident relief, got up again, went to look at himself in the mirror, ascertained that he was still himself (you never know), had a quick look inside the wardrobe, hung his cape up inside it, and then went over to the window.

"Are you part of the furniture, or did you just drop in?"

The youngster didn't move an inch. But he answered.

"Furniture."

"Ah."

Bartleboom returned toward the bed, loosened his cravat, and stretched out. Damp stains on the ceiling, like black and white drawings of tropical flowers. He closed his eyes and fell asleep. He dreamed that they had called him in to substitute for the fat lady with Bosendorf's Circus and, once in the ring, he recognized his aunt Adelaide in the first row. A delightful lady but one of debatable habits, she was kissing first a pirate, then a woman identical to herself, and finally the wooden statue of a saint that could not have been a statue for he was suddenly coming straight for him, Bartleboom, shouting something that he couldn't quite understand but sufficient nevertheless to arouse the indignation of all the spectators, so that he, Bartleboom, was obliged to take to his heels, and even to give up the rightful remuneration agreed upon with the manager of the circus, 128 soldi to be exact. He awoke, and the boy was still there. But he had turned around and was observing him. In fact, he was talking to him.

"Have you ever seen Bosendorf's Circus?"

"Pardon?"

"I asked you if you had ever seen Bosendorf's Circus."

Bartleboom sat bolt upright on the bed.

"What do you know of Bosendorf's Circus?"

"Nothing. I've only seen it, it passed through here last year. There were the animals and everything. There was the fat lady, too."

Bartleboom wondered whether he ought to inquire about Aunt Adelaide. True, she had been dead for years, but this lad seemed to know a thing or two. In the end he opted to get off the bed and walk over toward the window.

"Do you mind? I need a little air."

The boy moved over a little on the windowsill. Cold air and a north wind. Ahead, stretching to infinity, the sea.

"What do you do sitting up there all the time?"

"I look."

"There's not much to look at . . ."

"You're joking, aren't you?"

"Well, there is the sea, agreed, but then again the sea is never any different, it's always the same, sea as far as the horizon, on a good day a ship may pass by, but it's nothing to go overboard about, you know."

The boy turned toward the sea, turned back toward Bartle-boom, turned again toward the sea, and turned back again toward Bartleboom.

"How long are you going to stay here for?" he asked him.

"I don't know. A few days."

The boy got down from the windowsill, went toward the door, and stopped on the threshold, where he lingered a moment to regard Bartleboom.

"You're nice. Perhaps when you leave here you'll be a bit less of an imbecile."

Bartleboom felt a growing curiosity about who had brought up those children. A phenomenon, clearly.

EVENING. The Almayer Inn. The room on the first floor, at the end of the corridor. Writing desk, oil lamp, silence. A gray dressing gown with Bartleboom inside it. Two gray slippers with his feet inside them. A white sheet on the writing desk, a pen and an inkwell. He is writing, is Bartleboom. Writing.

My beloved,

I have arrived at the sea. I will spare you the trials and tribula-tions of the journey: what counts is that now I am here. The inn is hospitable: simple, but hospitable. It stands on the crest of a little hill, right in front of the beach. In the evenings the tide comes in and the water almost reaches a point below my window. It is like being on board a ship. You would like it.

I have never been on board a ship.

Tomorrow I shall begin my research. The place seems ideal to me. I am not unaware of the difficulties of my task, but you—you alone, in the world—know how determined I am to complete the work that it was my ambition to conceive and undertake one auspicious day twelve years ago. It will be of comfort to me to imagine you in health and in a cheerful state of mind.

As a matter of fact I had never thought about it before: but I really never have been on board a ship.

In the solitude of this place far removed from the world, I am accompanied by the certainty that you will not, far off as you are, mislay the memory of the one who loves you and will always remain your

Ismael A. Ismael Bartleboom.

He puts down the pen, folds the sheet of paper, and slips it inside an envelope. He stands up, takes from his trunk a mahogany box, lifts up the lid, lets the letter fall inside, open and unaddressed. In the box are hundreds of identical envelopes, open and unaddressed.

Bartleboom is thirty-eight. He thinks that somewhere in the world he will meet a woman who has always been *his* woman. Every now and again he regrets that destiny has been so stubbornly determined to make him wait with such indelicate tenacity, but with time he has learned to consider the matter with great serenity. Almost every day, for years now, he has taken pen in hand to write to her. He has no names or addresses to put on the envelopes: but he has a life to recount. And to whom, if not to her? He thinks that when they meet it will be wonderful to place a mahogany box full of letters on her lap and say to her, "I was waiting for you."

She will open the box and slowly, when she so desires, she will read the letters one by one, and as she works her way back up the interminable thread of blue ink she will gather up the years—the days, the moments—that that man, before he even met her, had already given to her. Or perhaps, more simply, she will overturn the box and, astonished at that comical snowstorm of letters, she will smile, saying to that man, "You are mad."

And she will love him forever.

~

CHAPTER 4

"FATHER PLUCHE..."

"Yes, my lord."

"Tomorrow my daughter will be fifteen years old."

"..."

"It has been eight years now since I entrusted her to your care."

"..."

"You have not cured her."

"No."

"She must take a husband."

"..."

"She must go out from this castle, and see the world."

"..."

"She must have children and . . ."

"..."

"In other words, she must begin to live, once and for all."

"..."

"..."

"..."

"Father Pluche, my daughter must be cured."

"Yes."

"Find someone who can cure her. And bring him here."

THE MOST FAMOUS DOCTOR in the land was called Atterdel. Many had seen him raise the dead, people who had one foot in the grave, already as good as gone, done for, really, and he had fished them back from Hell and brought them back to life, which was also an embarrassment if you will, sometimes even inconvenient, but it should be understood that that was his job, and no one could do it like he could, and so those people came back to life, *pace* friends and relatives all, who were obliged to start all over again, postponing tears and inheritances until better times, perhaps the next time they will consider things beforehand and seek the services of a normal doctor, one of those who does them in and that's that, not like this one who gets them back on their feet, only because he is the most famous doctor in the land. Not to mention the dearest.

And so Father Pluche thought of Dr. Atterdel. Not that he had much belief in doctors, it wasn't that, but for everything

22

that concerned Elisewin he was obliged to think with the Baron's head, not with his own. And the Baron's head thought that where God had failed, science might succeed. God had failed. Now it was up to Atterdel.

He arrived at the castle in a shiny black coach, which seemed somewhat sinister but was also very dramatic. He rapidly climbed the flight of steps, and when he came up to Father Pluche, almost without looking at him, asked, "Are you the Baron, sir?"

"I wouldn't half mind."

This was typical of Father Pluche. He was unable to restrain himself. He would never say what he ought to have said. Something else would come to mind first. Only a moment before. But it was more than enough time.

"Then, sir, you are Father Pluche."

"That's me."

"It was you who wrote to me."

"Yes."

"Well, you have a strange way of writing."

"In what sense?"

"There was no need to write everything in rhyme. I would have come in any case."

"Are you sure?"

For example: the right thing to say here was, "Excuse me, it was a silly game."

And in fact these words arrived all perfectly prepared in Father Pluche's head, all lined up in a nice neat row, but they came a fraction late, just enough time to be overtaken by a stupid gust of words that no sooner emerged on the surface of the silence than they crystallized into the incontrovertible brilliance of a question that was completely out of place.

"Are you sure?"

Atterdel looked up at Father Pluche. It was something more than a look. It was a medical examination.

"I am sure."

That's the good thing about men of science: they are sure.

"Where is this girl?"

"Yes ... Elisewin ... It's my name. Elisewin."

"Yes, Doctor."

"No, really, I'm not afraid. I always speak this way. It's my voice. Father Pluche says that . . ."

"Thank you, sir."

"I don't know. The oddest things. But it's not fear, not *real* fear . . . it's a bit different . . . fear comes from outside, I've understood this, there you are and fear *comes over* you, there's you and there's fear . . . that's how it is . . . there's fear and me too, but what happens to me is that suddenly *I'm not there anymore*, there's only the fear . . . which isn't really fear, though . . . I don't know what it is, do you know?"

"Yes, sir."

"Yes, sir."

"It's a bit like feeling you're dying. Or disappearing. That's it: *disappearing*. It seems as if your eyes are slipping away from your face, and your hands are becoming another's hands, and then you think what's happening to me?, and in the meantime your heart is beating inside you so hard you're dying for it to stop, it won't leave you in peace . . . and all over you feel as if parts of you were going away, you can't feel them anymore . . . you're on the point of going, and then I tell myself, think about something, you must hang on to a thought, if I can shrink into that thought then it will all pass, all you must do is resist, but the fact is that . . . and this is the really horrible thing . . . the fact is that *there are no thoughts anymore*, nowhere inside you, there is no thought any more but only *feelings*, do you see? Feelings . . . and the strongest of those is an infernal fever, and an intolerable stink, a taste of death here in the throat, a fever, and a bite, something that bites, a demon that is biting you and tearing you to pieces, a . . ."

"Excuse me, sir."

"Yes, there are times in which it is much . . . simpler, I mean, I feel myself disappearing, yes, but gently, very slowly . . . it's the emotions, Father Pluche says that it's the *emotions*, he says that I have nothing with which to defend myself against the emotions and so it's as if things entered directly through my eyes and my . . ."

"Through my eyes, yes."

"No, I don't remember. I know that I'm ill, but . . . sometimes there are things that don't frighten me, I mean, it's not always like that, the other night there was a terrible storm, lightning, wind . . . but I was calm, really, I wasn't afraid or anything . . . Other times all it takes is a color, maybe, or the form of an object, or . . . or the face of a man passing by, that's it, faces . . . faces can be terrible, can't they?—some faces, every so often, are so *real* that I feel they might set upon me, they are faces that scream, do you see what I mean?, they scream at you, it's horrible, there's no way to defend yourself, there's . . . no way . . ."

"*Love?*"

"Father Pluche reads me books, every now and again. They don't hurt me. My father would rather not, but . . . well, some stories also work on the *emotions*, do you see, with people who kill, who die . . . but I could listen to whatever came out of a book, that's the strange thing, I even manage to *cry* and it's a sweet thing, there is none of that stink of death, *I cry*, that's all, and Father Pluche carries on reading, and it's very nice, but my father mustn't know this, he doesn't know this, and perhaps it would be better if . . ."

"Of course I love my father. Why?"

"The white carpets?"

"I don't know."

"One day I saw my father sleeping. I went into his room and I saw him. My father. He was sleeping all curled up, like children do, on one side, with his legs drawn up, and his hands clenched into fists . . . I'll never forget it . . . my father, Baron Carewall. He was sleeping the way children do. Do you understand this, sir? How can you not be afraid if even . . . what can you do if even . . ."

"I don't know. No one ever comes here . . ."

"Sometimes. Yes, I notice. They talk quietly, when they are with me, and it also seems as if they move more . . . more *slowly*, as if they were afraid of breaking something. But I don't know if . . ."

"No, it's not difficult . . . it's *different*, I don't know, it's like being . . ."

"Father Pluche says that in reality I should have been a moth, but then there was a mistake, and so I came here, but it wasn't exactly here that I was supposed to land, and so now everything is a bit difficult, it's normal that everything makes me ill, I must have a lot of patience and wait, it's a complicated matter, you see, transforming a moth into a woman . . ."

"Very good, sir."

"But it's a kind of game, it's not exactly what you'd call a *true* thing, and it's not exactly *false*, either, if you knew Father Pluche . . ."

"Certainly, sir."

"An *illness*?"

"Yes."

"No, I'm not afraid. I'm not afraid of *that*, really."

"I shall do it."

"Yes."

"Yes."

"Good-bye, then."

". . . . ."

"Sir . . ."

"Sir, excuse me . . ."

"Sir, I wanted to say that I know I'm ill and I can't even manage to get out of here, from time to time, and for me, even running is too . . ."

"I wanted to say that I want life, I would do anything to have it, all the life there is, enough to drive me mad with it, it doesn't matter even if I do go mad, but I don't want to forgo life, I want it, really, I'm dying to live, even if it hurts. I'll be able to, won't I?"

"I will be able to, won't I?"

SINCE SCIENCE IS STRANGE, a strange beast, which seeks its lair in the most absurd places, and works according to meticulous plans that from the outside can only appear inscrutable and sometimes even comic, so much like aimless wanderings do they seem and instead they are geometrical hunting trails, traps laid with cunning art, and strategic battles before which one may stand astonished much as Baron Carewall stood astonished when that doctor dressed in black finally spoke to him, looking him in the eye, with cold certitude but also, one might have said, with a hint of *tenderness*, a complete absurdity, for a man of science and Dr. Atterdel in particular, but not completely incomprehensible if only one could see inside the head of Dr. Atterdel himself where the image of that big strong man—Baron Carewall—continually gave way to the image of one huddled upon his bed, lying there sleeping like a *baby*, the great, powerful Baron and the little baby, one inside the other, so that you couldn't tell them apart anymore, so that you ended up being moved, even if you were a real man of science, as was, incontrovertibly, Dr. Atterdel when, with cold certitude and also a hint of tenderness he looked Baron Carewall in the eye and said, "I can save your daughter, sir"— he can save my daughter—"but it will not be simple and in a certain sense it will also be tremendously risky"—risky?—"it is an experiment, we do not really know yet what effects it may have, we have seen it many times, but no one can really say . . ." And here we have the geometrical trap of science, the enigmatic hunting trails, the match that the man dressed in black will play against the creeping and impregnable malady of a little girl too fragile to live and too alive to die, a fantastic malady that nevertheless has an enemy, and it is a huge one, medically risky but magnificent, completely absurd if you think about it, so much so that even the man of science lowers his voice at the precise moment he utters the name before the Baron's unwavering gaze, nothing more than a word, but one that will save his daughter, or kill her, but more probably save her, a single word, but infinite, in its way, even magical, intolerably simple.

"The *sea*?"

Baron Carewall's gaze remained unwavering. As far as his lands extended, there was not in that instant any amazement more crystalline than that which was teetering in his heart.

"You, sir, will save my daughter with the *sea*?"

ALONE, in the middle of the beach, Bartleboom
observed. Barefoot, his trousers rolled up to prevent their getting wet, a large notebook under his
arm and a woolen cap on his head. Leaning slightly forward,
he observed the ground. He was studying the exact point at
which the wave, after it had broken about ten yards farther
back, stretched out, became a lake, then a mirror and an oily
patch, climbed back up the slight slope of the beach, and
finally stopped—its outermost edge trimmed with a delicate
perlage—where it hesitated a moment and finally, defeated,
attempted an elegant withdrawal, letting itself slip back along
the line of what seemed an easy retreat, but instead fell, prey to
the spongy greed of that sand, which, until then unwarlike,

suddenly awoke and, the brief rush of water thus routed, evaporated into nothingness.

Bartleboom observed.

Within the imperfect circle of his optical universe, the perfection of that oscillatory motion formulated promises doomed to be broken by the uniqueness of each individual wave. There was no way of stopping that continual alternation of creation and destruction. His eyes sought the ordered and describable truth of a certain and complete image, but instead they wound up chasing after the mobile indeterminacy of the coming and going that deceived and derided scientific inquiry.

It was annoying. Something had to be done. Bartleboom arrested his eyes. He trained them ahead of his feet, framing a patch of silent and motionless sand. And he decided to wait. He had to stop chasing that exhausting to-ing and fro-ing. If Mohammed will not go to the mountain, etcetera, etcetera, he thought. Sooner or later—within the frame of that gaze imagined to possess scientific rigor—there would arrive the exact outline, trimmed with foam, of the wave he was waiting for. And there it would be permanently impressed in his mind. And he would *understand*. This was the plan. With total abnegation, Bartleboom fell into an emotionless immobility, transforming himself, so to speak, into a neutral and infallible optical instrument. He was hardly breathing. The artificial silence of the laboratory fell over the fixed circle delimited by his gaze. He was like a trap, imperturbable and patient. He was waiting for his prey. And, slowly, his prey arrived. A pair of women's shoes. High, but women's shoes.

"You must be Bartleboom, sir."

Bartleboom had really been expecting a wave. Or something of that kind. He looked up and saw a woman, wrapped in an elegant purple cloak.

"Bartleboom, yes . . . Professor Ismael Bartleboom."

"Have you lost something?"

Bartleboom realized that he was still bent over forward, a frozen contour of the optical instrument he had transformed himself into. He straightened up with all the ease he was capable of. Very little indeed.

"No. I am working."

"Working?"

"Yes, I am . . . I am engaged in research, you see, research . . ."

"Ah."

"Scientific research, I mean to say . . ."

"Scientific."

"Yes."

Silence. The woman drew her purple cloak closer around her.

"Shells, lichens, things of that kind?"

"No. Waves."

Just like that: *waves.*

"That is . . . you see there, where the water arrives . . . runs up the beach, then stops . . . there, precisely that point, where it stops . . . it really lasts no more than an instant, look there, there, for example, there . . . you see that it lasts only an instant, then it disappears, but if one were to succeed in suspending that instant . . . when the water stops, precisely that

32

point, that curve . . . this is what I am studying. Where the water stops."

"And what is there to study?"

"Well, it's an important point . . . sometimes you hardly notice it, but if you think about, it something extraordinary happens at that point, something . . . extraordinary."

"Really?"

Bartleboom leaned slightly closer to the woman. One would have thought that he had a secret to tell when he said, "That is where the sea ends."

The immense sea, the ocean sea, which runs infinitely beyond all sight, the huge omnipotent sea—there is a point where it ends, and an instant—the immense sea, the tiniest place and a split second. This was what Bartleboom wanted to say.

The woman let her gaze run over the water that was slipping heedlessly to and fro across the sand. When she raised her eyes again to look at Bartleboom, they were smiling.

"My name is Ann Deverià."

"Most honored."

"I, too, am staying at the Almayer Inn."

"This is splendid news."

As usual, the north wind was blowing. The pair of women's shoes crossed what had been Bartleboom's laboratory and moved a few steps away. Then they stopped. The woman turned.

"Will you take tea with me this afternoon, sir?"

Bartleboom had seen some things only at the theater.

And at the theater they always answered:

"It will be a pleasure."

"AN ENCYCLOPEDIA of limits?"

"Yes . . . the full title is *An Encyclopedia of the Limits to be found in Nature with a Supplement devoted to the Limits of the Human Faculties.*"

"And you are writing it . . ."

"Yes."

"On your own."

"Yes."

"Milk?"

Bartleboom always took his tea with lemon.

"Yes, thank you . . . milk."

A cloud.

Sugar.

Teaspoon.

Teaspoon stirring the tea.

Teaspoon coming to rest.

Teaspoon in saucer.

Ann Deverià, sitting before him, listening.

"Nature is possessed of a surprising perfection, and this is the result of a sum of limits. Nature is perfect because it is not infinite. If you understand the limits, you understand how the mechanism works. It is all a matter of understanding the limits. Take rivers, for example. A river may be long, very long indeed, but it cannot be infinite. If the system is to work, the river must end. And I study how long it can be before it must end. Five hundred thirty-six miles. That is one of the entries I have already written: *Rivers*. It took me a good while, as you can well understand, Madame."

Ann Deverià understood.

"That is to say: the leaf of a tree, if you look at it carefully, is a very complex universe: but finite. The largest leaf is found in China: three feet nine inches broad, and more or less twice as long. Enormous, but not infinite. And there is an exact logic in this: a larger leaf could only grow on an immense tree, but the tallest tree, which grows in America, does not exceed two hundred fifty-eight feet, a considerable height, certainly, but entirely insufficient to support a number, even a limited one—because naturally it would be limited—of leaves larger than those found in China. Do you see the logic, Madame?"

Ann Deverià saw the logic.

"This is laborious research, and difficult, too, it cannot be denied, but it is important to understand. To describe. The last entry I wrote was *Sunsets*. You see, this thing about days *ending* is ingenious. It is an ingenious system. The days and then the nights. And then the days again. It would seem something to be expected, but there is genius in it. And at the point where Nature decides to set her own limits, the spectacle explodes. Sunsets. I studied them for weeks. It is not easy to *understand* a sunset. It has its own times, its dimensions, its colors. And since there is not one sunset, not one I say, that is identical to another, then the scientist must be able to discern the details and isolate the essence to the point where he may say 'this is a sunset.' Am I boring you, Madame?"

Ann Deverià was not bored. That is, no more than usual.

"And so now I have come to the sea. The sea. The sea ends, too, like everything else, but you see, here, too, it is a little like sunsets, the hard thing is to isolate the idea, I mean to say, to condense miles and miles of cliffs, shores, and beaches, into a single image, into a concept that is *the end of the sea*, something you may set down in a few lines, that may have a place in an encyclopedia, so that people, upon reading it, may understand that the sea ends, and how, independently of everything that may happen around it, independently of . . ."

"Bartleboom . . ."

"Yes?"

"Ask me why *I* am here."

Silence. Embarrassment.

"I haven't asked you, have I?"

"Ask me now."

"Why are you here, Madame Deverià?"

"To be cured."

More embarrassment, more silence. Bartleboom takes the cup, brings it to his lips. Empty. Forget it. He puts it down again.

"To be cured of what?"

"It is a strange malady. Adultery."

"I beg your pardon?"

"Adultery, Bartleboom. I have betrayed my husband. And my husband thinks that the sea air may cool the passions, and that the sight of the sea may stimulate the ethical sense, and that the solitude of the sea may induce me to forget my lover."

"Really?"

"Really what?"

"Did you really betray your husband?"

"Yes."

"A drop more tea?"

PERCHED ON the last narrow ledge of the world, a stone's throw from the end of the sea, that evening, too, the Almayer Inn let the darkness gradually silence the colors of its walls, and of the whole world and the entire ocean. So alone was it there, it seemed a thing forgotten. It was almost as if a procession of inns, of every kind and vintage, had passed by there one day, skirting the coast, when, out of tiredness, one had detached itself from the rest, and, as its traveling companions filed past, it decided to stop on that slight rise, yielding to its own weakness, bowing its head and waiting for the end. The Almayer Inn was like that. It had that beauty of which only the defeated are capable. And the clarity of frail things. And the perfect solitude of the lost.

Plasson, the painter, had only recently returned, sopping wet, with his canvases and his paints, seated in the bow of the rowboat, propelled by a young lad with red hair.

"Thank you, Dol. See you tomorrow."

"Good night, Monsieur Plasson."

How it was Plasson had not already died of pneumonia was a mystery. A man cannot stand for hours and hours in the north wind, with his feet soaking and the tide creeping up his trousers, without dying sooner or later.

"First he has to finish his picture," Dira had announced.

"He will never finish it," said Madame Deverià.

"Then he'll never die."

In room number 3, on the first floor, an oil lamp illuminated Professor Ismael Bartleboom at his ritual devotions, softly revealing their secret to the surrounding evening.

My beloved,

God knows how I miss, in this melancholy hour, the comfort of your presence and the balm of your smiles. My work fatigues me and the sea rebels against my stubborn attempts to understand it. I had not thought it could be so difficult to face. And I wander about, with my instruments and my notebooks, without finding the beginning of that which I seek, the access to any sort of answer. Where does the end of the sea begin? Or, indeed, what are we saying when we say sea? Do we mean the immense monster capable of devouring absolutely anything, or the wave foaming around our feet? The water you can hold in a cupped hand, or the abyss that none can see? Do we say everything with a single word, or with a single word do we conceal everything? I am here, a stone's throw from the sea, and I cannot even understand where it is. The sea. The sea.

Today I met a most beautiful woman. But be not jealous. I live only for you.

Ismael A. Ismael Bartleboom

Bartleboom wrote with a serene facility, without ever stopping and with a slowness that nothing could have disturbed. He liked to think that, one day, she would caress him the same way.

In the half-light, with the long, slim fingers that had driven more than one man mad, Ann Deverià toyed with the pearls of her necklace—a rosary of desire—in the unconscious gesture she always made when sad. She watched the guttering flame of the oil lamp, glancing from time to time in the mirror, where the struggles of those desperate little glimmers of light sketched her face over and over. Leaning into those last little surges of light, she went over to the bed where, under the covers, a little girl slept all unaware of any other place; she was most beautiful. Ann Deverià looked at her, but with a look for which the word *look* is too strong, a marvelous look that is seeing without wondering about anything, seeing and no more, something like two things that touch each other—the eyes and the image—a look that does not *take* but *receives*, in the absolute silence of the mind, the *only* look that could really save us—innocent of any question, still not tainted by the vice of *wanting to know*—the only innocence that could prevent the hurt caused by external things when they enter the sphere of our sensibilities—to see—to feel—because it would be no more than a marvelous *vis-à-vis*, us and things, whereby our eyes *receive* the whole world—to receive—without questions, even without wonder—to receive—only—to receive—in our eyes—the world. A way of seeing known only to the eyes of the Madonnas, as, under the vaults of the churches, they watch the angel descend from skies of gold at the hour of the Annunciation.

Darkness. Ann Deverià tightly embraces the little girl's unclothed body, within the secret of her bed, plump with covers light as clouds. Her fingers run lightly across that incredible skin, and her lips search in the most hidden folds for the bland flavor of sleep. She moves slowly, Ann Deverià. A dance in slow motion, an adagio that loosens something in the head and between the legs and all over. There is no dance more precise than that, waltzing with sleep on the parquet of the night.

The last light, in the last window, goes out. Only the unstoppable machine of the sea still tears away at the silence with the cyclical explosion of nocturnal waves, distant memories of sleepwalking storms and the shipwrecks of dream.

Night over the Almayer Inn.

Motionless night.

BARTLEBOOM AWOKE TIRED and in a bad mood. For hours, in sleep, he had negotiated the purchase of Chartres cathedral with an Italian cardinal, and in the end had obtained a monastery in the vicinity of Assisi at the exorbitant price of sixteen thousand crowns plus a night with his cousin Dorothea and a quarter-share of the Almayer Inn. The deal, in addition, had been struck aboard a boat perilously at the mercy of the waves and commanded by a gentleman who claimed he was Madame Deverià's husband and, laughing—*laughing*—admitted he knew nothing whatsoever about the sea. When he awoke, he was exhausted. He was not surprised to see, straddling the windowsill, the usual boy who, motionless, was looking at the sea. But he was distinctly surprised to hear him say, without even turning around, "Me, I would have told him what to do with his monastery."

Bartleboom got out of bed and, without a word, took the boy by the arm, dragged him down from the windowsill, then out the door, and finally downstairs, shouting, "Miss Dira!" as he rolled down the stairs to arrive finally on the ground floor where—"MISS DIRA!"—he finally found what he was looking for, that is, the reception desk—if we can call it that—and, in short, he arrived, clutching the boy close to him all the while, in the presence of Miss Dira—ten years old, not a year more—where he stopped, finally, with a proud demeanor only partly undermined by the human frailty of his yellow nightshirt, and more seriously undermined by the combination of that garment with a woolen nightcap, open mesh knit.

Dira looked up from her accounts. The two—Bartleboom and the boy—were standing at attention before her. They spoke one after the other, as if they had rehearsed their parts.

"This boy reads your dreams."

"This man talks in his sleep."

Dira lowered her gaze to her accounts once more. She did not even raise her voice.

"Scat."

They scatted.

CHAPTER 6

BECAUSE BARON CAREWALL had never seen the sea. His lands were land: stones, hills, marshes, fields, crags, mountains, woods, glades. Land. There was no sea.

For him the sea was an idea. Or, more correctly, an itinerary of the imagination. It was something born in the Red Sea—divided in two by the hand of God—then amplified by the thought of the Deluge, in which it was lost, to be found later in the bulging outline of an Ark and immediately connected to the thought of whales—never seen but often imagined—and thence it streamed back, fairly clear once more, into the few stories that had reached his ears of monstrous fish and dragons and submerged cities, in a crescendo of fantastic splendor that abruptly shriveled up into the harsh features of one of his forebears—framed and eternal in the gallery—who was said to have been a freebooter with Vasco da Gama: in his subtly wicked eyes, the thought of the sea took a sinister turn, caromed off some uncertain chronicles of piratical hyperbole, got entangled in a quotation from Saint Augustine according to which the ocean was the home of the devil, turned back to a name—Thessala—that was perhaps a wrecked ship or a wet-nurse who used to spin yarns of ships and wars, nearly surfaced in the redolence of certain cloths that had arrived there from distant lands, and finally reemerged in the eyes of a woman from overseas, encountered many years before and never seen since, to come to a halt, at the end of this circumnavigation of the mind, in the fragrance of a fruit that, they had told him, grew only along the seashore of the southern lands: and if you ate it you tasted the flavor of the sun. Since Baron Carewall had never seen it, the sea journeyed in his mind like a stowaway aboard a sailing ship moored in port with sails furled: inoffensive and superfluous.

It could have remained there forever. But, in an instant, it was aroused by the words of a man dressed in black called Atterdel, the verdict of an implacable man of science called in to make a miracle.

"I will save your daughter, sir. And I will do it with the *sea*."

In THE SEA. It was hard to believe. The polluted and putrid sea, receptacle of horrors, and anthropophagous monster

43

of the abyss—ancient and pagan—ever feared and now, suddenly

they invite you, as if for a walk, they order you, because it is a cure, they push you with implacable courtesy

into the sea. It is a fashionable cure, by now. A sea preferably cold, very salty, and choppy, because the dreadful content of the waves is an integral part of the cure, to be overcome technically and dominated morally, in a fearful challenge that is, if you think about it, fearful. And all in the certainty—let's say the conviction—that the great womb of the sea may sunder the outer shell of the malady, reactivate the pathways of life, increase the redeeming secretions of the central and peripheral glands

the ideal liniment for the hydrophobic, the melancholy, the impotent, the anemic, the lonely, the wicked, the envious,

and the mad. Like the madman they took to Brixton, under the impermeable gaze of doctors and scientists, and forcibly immersed in the gelid water, shaken violently by the waves, and then dragged out again and, reactions and counterreactions having been measured, again immersed, forcibly, let it be well understood,

eight degrees centigrade, his head under the water, he resurfacing like a scream and the brute force with which he frees himself of nurses and various personnel, excellent swimmers all, but this is absolutely useless in the face of the blind frenzy of the animal, who flees—flees—running through the water, nude, and screaming out the frenzy of that unbearable anguish, the shame, the terror. The entire beach frozen by the worrying disturbance, while that animal runs and runs, and the women, from far off, avert their gaze, although certainly they would like to see, and how they would like to see, the beast and his running, and let's face it, his nudity, yes his nudity, his rambling nudity stumbling blindly in the sea, even beautiful in that gray light, of a beauty that perforates years of good manners and boarding schools and blushes to go straight where it has to go, running along the nerve paths of timid women who, in the secrecy of enormous immaculate skirts

women. The sea suddenly seemed to have been waiting for them forever. To listen to the doctors, it had been there, for millennia, patiently perfecting itself, with the sole and precise intention of offering itself as a miraculous unguent for their afflictions of body and soul. Just as, while sipping tea in impeccable drawing rooms, impeccable doctors—weighing their words well in order to explain with paradoxical courtesy—would tell impeccable husbands and fathers over and over that the disgust for the sea, and the shock, and the terror, was in reality a seraphic cure for sterility, anorexia, nervous exhaustion, menopause, overexcitement, anxiety, and insomnia. An ideal experience inasmuch as it was a remedy for the ferments of youth and a preparation for wifely duties. A solemn baptism for young ladies become women. So that, if we wish to forget, for a moment, the madman in the sea at Brixton

(the madman carried on running, but out to sea, until he was lost to view, a scientific exhibit that

45

had eluded the statistics of the medical school to consign itself spontaneously to the belly of the ocean sea)

                                     if we wish to
forget him

          (digested by the great aquatic intestine and never
returned to the beach, never spewed back into the world,
as one might have expected, reduced to a shapeless, bluish
bladder)

       we could think of a woman—of a woman—respected,
loved, mother, woman. For whatever reason—*illness*—brought
to a sea that she would otherwise never have seen and that
is now the wavering needle of her cure, an immeasurable
index, in truth, which she contemplates but does not understand. Her hair hangs loose and she is barefoot, and this is
not a mere detail, it is absurd, along with that little white
tunic and the trousers that leave her ankles exposed, you
could imagine her slim hips, it is absurd, only her boudoir
has seen her like this, and yet, like that, there she is on an
enormous beach, where there is none of the viscous, stagnant
air of the bridal bed, but the gusty sea breeze bearing the edict
of a wild freedom removed, forgotten, oppressed, debased for
a whole lifetime as mother, wife, beloved woman. And it is
clear: she cannot not feel it. That emptiness all around, with
no walls or closed doors, and in front of her, alone, a boundless exciting mirror of water, that alone would already have
been a feast for the senses, an orgy of the nerves, and
everything is yet to happen, the bite of the gelid water, the
fear, the liquid embrace of the sea, the shock on the skin,
the heart in the mouth . . .

She is accompanied toward the water. Over her face there falls a sublime concealment, a silken mask.

On the other hand, no one ever came to claim the corpse of the madman of Brixton. This has to be said. The doctors were experimenting, this must be understood. Some unbelievable couples were walking around, the patient and his doctor, delicate invalids of exquisite elegance, devoured by a disease of divine slowness, and doctors like rats in a cellar, seeking clues, evidence, numbers, and figures: scrutinizing the movements of the disease in its bewildered flight from the ambush of a paradoxical cure. They were *drinking* the sea water, things had gone that far, the water that until the day before had been horror and disgust, and the privilege of a forlorn and barbarous humanity, skin burned by the sun, humiliating foulness. Now they were *sipping* it, those same divine invalids who walked along the water's edge imperceptibly dragging one leg, in an extraordinary simulation of a noble lameness that might exempt them from the everyday commonplace whereby one foot is to be placed in front of the other. Everything was the cure. Some found a wife, others wrote poems, it was the same world as ever—repugnant, if you think about it—that had suddenly been transferred, *for wholly medical purposes,* to the edge of an abyss abhorred for centuries and now chosen, out of choice and in the cause of science, as the promenade of suffering.

The *wave bath,* the doctors called it. There was even a machine, really, a kind of patented sedan chair for getting into the sea, it was for the ladies, obviously, ladies and young ladies,

47

to protect them from indiscreet eyes. They would board the sedan chair, closed on all sides by curtains in muted colors, and then they would be carried into the sea, for a few yards' distance, and there, with the sedan chair almost touching the water, they would step down and take the bath, as if it were a medicine, almost invisible behind their curtains, curtains in the wind, sedan chairs like floating tabernacles, curtains like the vestments of a ceremony inexplicably lost on the water; from the beach it was a sight to be seen. The wave bath.

Only science *can do* certain things, this is the truth. To sweep away centuries of disgust—the horrendous sea womb of corruption and death—and invent that idyll that little by little spreads to all the beaches of the

world. Healing like

love. And now this: one day on the beach at Depper a wave washed up a boat, ruined, little more than a wreck. And there they were, those who had been seduced by illness, scattered along the interminable beach, each one immersed in his marine coitus, elegant traceries on the sand as far as the eye could see, each one in his own bubble of emotion, lust, and fear. Regardless of the science that had called them there, each one descended from his heaven to pace slowly toward the wreck that hesitated to run aground in the sand, like a messenger fearful of arriving. They came closer. They pulled it up onto the sand. And they saw. Laid out on the bottom of the boat, with gaze upturned and arm outstretched to proffer something that was there no longer, they saw:

a saint. It was made of wood, the statue. Colored. The mantle fell as far as the feet, a wound ran across the throat, but the face, the face knew nothing about this and it reposed, meek, on a bed of divine serenity. Nothing else in the boat, only the saint. Alone. And everybody instinctively raised his eyes, for a moment, to scan the surface of the ocean for the outline of a church, an understandable idea but also an irrational one, there were no churches, there were no crosses, there were no paths, the sea is trackless, the sea is without explanations.

The gaze of dozens of invalids, and beautiful, distant, consumptive women, the ratlike doctors, assistants, and valets, old peeping Toms, the curious, fishermen, young girls—and *a saint*. Bewildered, all of them and him. Suspended.

On the beach at Depper, one day.

No one ever understood.

Ever.

"YOU WILL TAKE HER to Daschenbach, sir, it is an ideal beach for the wave bath. Three days. One immersion in the morning and one in the afternoon. Ask for Dr. Taverner, he will procure you all that is necessary. This is a letter of introduction for him. Take it."

The Baron took the letter without even looking at it.

"She will die of it," he said.

"It is possible. But highly improbable."

Only great doctors can be so cynically precise.

Atterdel was the *greatest*.

"Let me put it this way, my lord: you can keep that little girl in here for years, to walk on white carpets and sleep among flying men. But one day an emotion you cannot foresee will carry her off. Amen. Or you can accept the risk, follow my orders, and trust in God. The sea will give you back your daughter. Dead, perhaps. But if alive, then really alive."

Cynically precise.

The Baron had remained motionless, with the letter in his hand, halfway between him and the doctor dressed in black.

"You have no children, sir."

"That is a fact of no importance."

"But nevertheless you have no children."

He looked at the letter and slowly placed it on the table.

"Elisewin shall remain here."

A moment of silence, but only a moment.

"Not on your life."

This was Father Pluche. In reality the phrase that had set out from his brain was more complex and closer to something like "Perhaps it would be better to postpone any decision until after having serenely reflected upon that which . . .": something like that. But "Not on your life" was clearly a nimbler, quicker statement, and it was no great effort for it to slip through the net of the other one and bob up onto the surface of the silence like an unforeseen and unforeseeable buoy.

"Not on your life."

It was the first time in sixteen years that Father Pluche had dared to contradict the Baron in a question pertinent to Elisewin's life. He felt a strange inebriation, as if he had just thrown himself out of a window. He was a man with a certain practical spirit: given that he was already up in the air, he decided to try to take flight.

"Elisewin shall go to the sea. I shall take her there. And if need be we shall stay there for months, years, until she manages to find the strength to face the water and everything else. And in the end she shall return—alive. Any other decision would be idiotic or, worse, base. And though Elisewin is afraid, we must not be, and I shall not be. She cares nothing about dying. She wants to live. And what she wants, she shall have."

It was hard to believe the way Father Pluche spoke. Hard to believe it was him.

"You sir, Dr. Atterdel, you understand nothing of men and of fathers and children, nothing. And that's why I believe you. The truth is always inhuman. Like you, sir. I know that you are not mistaken. I pity you, but I admire your words. And I who have never seen the sea, to the sea I shall go, because your words have told me to do so. It is the most absurd, ridiculous, and senseless thing that I might be called upon to undertake. But there is no man, in all of Carewall, who could stop me from doing it. No one."

He picked the letter up from the table and put it in his pocket. His heart was thumping like mad, his hands were shaking, and there was a strange buzzing in his ears. Nothing surprising about that, he thought: it's not every day you take flight.

Anything could have happened in that moment. There really are times when the omnipresent and logical network of causal sequences gives up, taken unawares by life, and climbs down into the stalls to mingle with the public, so that up on the stage, under the lights of a sudden, dizzying freedom, an invisible hand may fish in the infinite womb of the possible and, out of millions of things, will permit one thing alone to happen. In the silent triangle formed by those three men, all the millions of things that could have exploded into being passed by in succession, but in a flash, until, the glare having faded and the dust settled, one sole, minute thing appeared, within the sphere of that time and space, struggling with a certain modest reserve to happen. And it happened. The Baron—the Baron of Carewall—began to cry, without even hiding his face in his hands, but merely letting himself slump back against the back of his sumptuous seat, as if defeated by fatigue, but also as if freed of an enormous burden. Like a dead man but also like a man who had been saved.

Baron Carewall cried.

Cried his eyes out.

Father Pluche, motionless.

Dr. Atterdel, speechless.

And that was it.

THESE WERE all things that no one ever came to know of in Carewall. But everyone, without exception, still tells of what happened *afterwards*. The sweetness of what happened afterwards.

"Elisewin . . ."

"A miraculous cure . . ."

"The sea. . . ."

"It is madness . . . ."

"She will get better, you'll see."

"She will die."

"The sea . . . ."

The sea, as the Baron saw from the geographer's charts, was far away. But above all—he saw in his dreams—it was terrible, exaggeratedly beautiful, terribly powerful, inhuman and inimical: marvelous. Marvelous colors, odors never perceived, sounds unknown—it was another world. He would look at Elisewin and could not imagine how she could get close to all that without disappearing into nothingness, dispersed in the air by the commotion and the surprise. He thought of the moment when she would turn, suddenly, and her gaze would receive the sea. He thought about it for weeks. And then he understood. It was not difficult, at bottom. It was incredible that he had not thought of it before.

"How shall we get to the sea?" Father Pluche asked him.

"It shall be the sea that comes to get you."

And so they left, one April morning. They crossed fields and hills and at sunset on the fifth day they reached the banks of a river. There was no town, there were no houses, nothing. But on the water, silent, there swayed a little ship. She was called the *Adel*. She usually sailed the waters of the Ocean, carrying wealth and want to and fro between the continent and the islands. On the prow was a figurehead whose hair flowed from head to foot. The sails held all the winds of the faraway world. The keel had been observing the womb of the sea for years. In every nook, unknown odors told the stories that the sailors wore transcribed on their skin. She was a two-master.

Baron Carewall had commanded her to follow the course of the river from the sea to that point.

"It is folly," the captain had written to him.

"I shall shower you with gold," the Baron had replied.

And now, like a phantasm departing from any reasonable course, the two-master known as the *Adel* was there. On the little quay, where only insignificant little craft were usually moored, the Baron clasped his daughter to him and said, "Adieu."

Elisewin said nothing. She covered her face with a silken veil, slipped a folded and sealed sheet of paper into her father's hands, turned, and went toward the men who would take her on board. It was almost night by then. It could have been a dream.

And so Elisewin went down to the sea in the gentlest way possible—only a father's mind could have thought of it— borne by the current, along the bends, pauses, and hesitations that the river had learned in centuries of journeying; a great sage, the river was the only one who knew the gentlest, mildest, most beautiful way one could get to the sea without harming oneself. They went down the river, with that slowness determined precisely by the maternal wisdom of nature, slipping gradually into a world of odors and colored things that, day after day, revealed, with extreme slowness, the presence, at first distant and then ever nearer, of the enormous womb that awaited them. The air changed, the dawns changed, and the skies, and the shapes of the houses, and the birds, and the sounds, and the faces of the people, on the banks, and the words of the people in their mouths. Water slipping toward water, a most delicate courtship, the bends of the river like a lullaby of the soul. An imperceptible journey. In Elisewin's mind, sensations by the thousand, but as weightless as feathers in flight.

Still today, in Carewall, everyone tells the tale of that journey. Each one in his own way. And all without ever having seen it. But this does not matter. They will never stop telling it. So that no one may forget how fine it would be if, for each sea that awaits us, there were a river, for us. And someone— a father, a lover, someone—capable of taking us by the hand and finding that river—imagining it, inventing it—and placing us on its flow with the buoyancy of a single word, adieu. This, really, would be marvelous. Life would be *sweet*, any life. And things would not do harm but, borne on the current, they would come closer; first one could get very close to them and then touch them and only at the end let oneself be touched by them. Let oneself be *hurt* by them, even. *Die of them.* It does not matter. But everything would be, finally, *human*. All that is needed is someone's imagination—a father, a lover, someone. He would be able to invent a way, here, in the midst of this silence, in this land that will not speak. A clement way, and a beautiful one. A way from here to the sea.

BOTH MOTIONLESS, eyes fixed on that immense stretch of water. Unbelievable. Really. You could stay there for a lifetime, understanding nothing, but still looking. The sea ahead, a long river behind, and finally the ground beneath one's feet. And those two there, motionless. Elisewin and Father Pluche.

Like a spell. Without so much as a thought in their heads, a real thought, only amazement. Wonder. And it is only after minutes and minutes—an eternity—that Elisewin, finally, without taking her eyes off the sea, says, "But then, at a certain point, does it end?"

Hundreds of miles away, in the solitude of his enormous castle, a man holds a sheet of paper close to a candle and reads. Few words, all on one line. Black ink.

Do not be afraid. I am not. I who love you. Elisewin.

The carriage will pick them up, then, because it is evening, and the inn awaits them. A short journey. The road that skirts the beach. All around, no one. Almost no one. In the sea— what's he doing *in* the sea?—a painter.

CHAPTER 7

~

I N SUMATRA, off the north coast of Pangei, every
seventy-six days there would emerge an island in the form
of a cross, covered with lush vegetation and apparently
uninhabited. It would remain visible for a few hours before
plunging back beneath the sea. On the beach at Cascais the
local fishermen had found the remains of the ship *Davemport*,
wrecked eight days before, on the other side of the world,
in the Ceylon sea. On the route for Farhadhar, mariners used
to see strange luminous butterflies that induced stupefaction
and a sense of melancholy. In the waters of Bogador, a convoy
of four naval vessels had disappeared, devoured by a single
enormous wave that had appeared out of nowhere on a day of
flat calm.

Admiral Langlais leafed slowly through those documents that arrived from the farthest-flung corners of a world that evidently clung to its follies. Letters, extracts from ships' logs, newspaper clippings, police reports, confidential reports, embassy dispatches. All sorts of things. The lapidary coldness of official communiqués or the alcoholic confidences of visionary seamen all crossed the world just the same to arrive on that desk where, in the name of the Realm, Langlais would take his goose-quill pen and trace the boundary between that which, in the Realm, would be considered true and that which would be forgotten as false. From the seas of the world, hundreds of statistics and rumors arrived in procession on that desk to be swallowed up by a verdict as fine as a thread of black ink, embroidered with a precise hand on leatherbound books. Langlais's hand was the womb in which they all went to lay their journeys to rest. His pen, the blade beneath which their labors bared their necks. A clean, precise death.

THIS PRESENT INFORMATION *is to be held as unfounded, and as such it is forbidden to divulge it or cite it in the charts and documents of the Realm.*

OR, FOREVER, a serene life.

THIS PRESENT INFORMATION *is to be held as veracious, and as such will appear in all the charts and documents of the Realm.*

He would judge, Langlais. He would compare the evidence, weigh up the testimony, investigate the sources. And then he would judge. He lived in daily contact with the specters of an immense collective fantasy where the clear gaze of the explorer and the haunted look of the shipwrecked produced images that were sometimes identical, and tales that were illogically complimentary. He lived among marvels. For this reason a preestablished and maniacal order reigned in his house while his life flowed along in accordance with an immutable geometry of habits that came close to the holiness of a liturgy. He defended himself, did Langlais. He bound up his own existence with a web of extremely elaborate rules capable of cushioning the dizzying effects of the images to which, every day, he opened his mind. The hyperboles that reached him from all the seas of the world subsided against the meticulous dike delineated by those minute certainties. One step farther on, the placid lake that was Langlais's wisdom awaited them. Still and just.

From the open window there came the rhythmic sound of the gardener's shears as he pruned the roses with the certainty of Justice intent on handing down redeeming verdicts. A sound like any other. But that day, and in Admiral Langlais's head, that sound communicated a decidedly precise message. Patient and obstinate—too close to the window to be accidental—in it could be heard the memory of a commitment. Langlais would have preferred not to listen to it. But he was a man of honor. And so he laid aside the pages that told of islands, wrecks, and butterflies, opened a drawer, took out three sealed letters and placed them on the desk. They came from three different places. Although they bore the distinguishing marks of urgent confidential correspondence, Langlais, out of baseness, had let them lie for several days in a place where he could not even see them. But now he opened them with a crisp, formal gesture, and forbidding himself any hesitation, he set to reading them. On a leaf of paper he noted down some names, a date. He tried to do everything with the impersonal neutrality of a royal accountant. The last note he took read

The Almayer Inn, Quartel

Finally he picked up the letters and got up and went to the fireplace, where he threw them into the prudent flames that kept watch over the indolent spring of those days. While he was watching the fire crumple the affected elegance of those missives that he had never wished to read, he distinctly perceived a sudden and thankful silence from the open window. The shears, until then as tireless as the hands of a watch, had fallen silent. Only after a little did the gardener's footsteps engrave themselves in the silence as he moved away. There was something precise about that departure that would have amazed anyone. But not Langlais. He knew. Mysterious for anyone else, the relationship that linked those two men—an admiral and a gardener—no longer held any secrets for them. The custom of a familiarity made up of many silences and private signals had guarded their singular alliance for years.

There are many stories. That one came from long before.

ONE DAY, six years previously, they had brought into the presence of Admiral Langlais a man who, they said, was named Adams. Tall, robust, long hair hanging down to his shoulders, skin burned by the sun. He might have seemed a seaman like so many others. But they had to hold him up; he was unable to walk. A disgusting ulcerated wound marked his neck. He remained absurdly motionless, as if paralyzed, absent. The only thing that suggested some vestiges of awareness was his gaze. It looked like the gaze of a dying animal.

He has the look of an animal stalking its prey, thought Langlais.

They said that they had found him in a village in the heart of Africa. There were also other white men down there: slaves. But he was something different. He was the tribal chieftain's favorite animal. He would stand on all fours, grotesquely decorated with feathers and colored stones, tied by a rope to the king's throne. He would eat the scraps that the king threw to him. His body was tormented by cuts and blows. He had learned to bark in a way that amused the sovereign hugely. If he was still alive, that was probably the only reason why.

"What does he have to say?" asked Langlais.

"Him? Nothing. He doesn't talk. He doesn't want to talk. But those that were with him—the other slaves—and also those who recognized him, at the harbor . . . well, they tell some extraordinary tales about him; it's as if he had been everywhere, this man, he is a mystery . . . If you were to believe all they say . . ."

"*What* do they say?"

He, Adams, motionless and absent, in the middle of the room. And all around him the bacchanal of memory and fantasy that exploded and frescoed the air with the adventures of a life that, they said, was his / three hundred miles on foot in the desert / he swears that he saw him change into a Negro and then become white again / because he trafficked with the local shaman, it was there that he learned how to make that red powder which / when they captured them they tied them all to one huge tree and waited until the insects had covered them completely, but he began to speak in an incomprehensible tongue and it was then that those savages, suddenly / swearing that he had climbed those mountains where the light never disappears, and that's why no one had ever returned sane from there, except for him, who, when he came back, said only / at the Sultan's court, where he had been taken thanks to his voice, which was beautiful, and he, covered with gold, had to stand in the torture chamber and sing while they went about their work, and all so that the Sultan would not hear the disagreeable echo of the cries of the tortured but rather the beauty of that song which / on Lake Kalabaki, which is as big as the sea, and there they believed that it was the sea, until they built a boat out of enormous leaves, the leaves of a tree, and used it to sail from one shore to the other, and he was aboard that boat, I could swear to it / prospecting for diamonds in the sand, by hand, chained and naked, so that they could not escape, and he was in the middle of them, just as it's true that / they all said that he was dead, carried off by the storm, but one day they were cutting the hands off a man, before the Tesfa Gate, a water thief, and so I had a good look, and it was him, yes, him / and that's why he calls himself Adams, but he has had a thousand names and one fellow, once, met him when he was known as Ra Me Nivar, which, in the language of that place, meant The Man Who Flies, and another time, on the African coasts / in the city of the dead, where no one dared enter, because there was a centuries-old curse, which made the eyes explode of all those who

"That will do."

Langlais did not even raise his eyes from the tobacco jar that he had been nervously toying with for some minutes.

"Very well. Take him away."

Nobody moved.

Silence.

"Admiral . . . there is another thing."

"What?"

Silence.

"This man has seen Timbuktu."

Langlais's tobacco jar became still.

"There are people prepared to swear to it: he has been there."

Timbuktu. The pearl of Africa. The marvelous city that may not be found. The chest of all treasures, the home of all barbarian gods. The heart of the unknown world, the citadel of a thousand secrets, the fantastic realm of all wealth, the lost destination of infinite journeys, the source of all waters and the dream of any heaven. Timbuktu. The city that no white man had ever found.

Langlais looked up. Everybody in the room seemed enthralled by a sudden immobility. Only Adams's eyes continued to roam, intent on stalking an invisible prey.

THE ADMIRAL QUESTIONED HIM for a long time. As was his habit, he spoke with a voice that was severe but mild, almost impersonal. Only a patient procession of brief, precise questions. He did not obtain a single answer.

Adams kept silent. He seemed forever exiled to a world that was inexorably elsewhere. Langlais did not even wrest a glance from him. Nothing.

Langlais stood there staring at him in silence for a while. Then he made a gesture that admitted of no objections. They heaved Adams up from the chair and dragged him away. Langlais watched him as he departed—his feet dragging on the marble floor—and had the unpleasant sensation that, in that moment, on the approximative charts in the possession of the Realm, Timbuktu was also slipping farther and farther away. For no reason, one of the many legends surrounding that city came to mind: that the women, down there, kept only one eye uncovered, wonderfully painted with colored earth. He had always wondered why ever it was that they should hide the other eye. He got up and idly moved over to the window. He was thinking of opening it when a voice, in his head, froze him as it pronounced a clear, precise phrase:

"Because no one could hold their gaze without going mad."

Langlais whirled around. There was no one in the room. He turned back toward the window. For a few moments he was unable to think of anything at all. Then he saw, filing by in the avenue below, the little escort that was taking Adams back to nothingness. He did not wonder what he should have done. He simply did it.

A few moments later he was standing before Adams, surrounded by the amazement of the onlookers and slightly wearied after the fast run. He looked him in the eyes and in a low voice said, "And you, how do you know?"

Adams did not seem to have even noticed him. He was still in some strange place, thousands of miles from there. But his lips moved and they all heard his voice say, "Because I have seen them."

LANGLAIS HAD COME across many cases like that of Adams. Sailors whom a storm or the cruelty of pirates had hurled onto the coast of an unknown continent, hostages to chance and the prey of peoples for whom the white man was little more than a bizarre animal species. If a kind death did not take them swiftly, it was one kind of atrocious death or another that awaited them in some fetid or marvelous corner of incredible worlds. Few were those who came out of such situations alive, picked up by some ship and reconsigned to the civilized world bearing the irreversible mark of their catastrophe. Mindless wrecks, human detritus returned from the unknown. Lost souls.

Langlais knew all this. And yet he took Adams with him. He stole him from wretchedness and took him into his palace. In whatever world his mind had gone to hide, there he would go to find it. And he would bring it back. He did not want to save him. It was not exactly like that. He wanted to save the stories that were hidden inside him. It did not matter how much time it would take: he wanted those stories, and he would have them.

He knew that Adams was a man destroyed by his own life. In his mind's eye, Adams's soul was a peaceful village sacked and dispersed by the savage invasion of a dizzying number of images, sensations, odors, sounds, pains, words. The death he simulated, to look at him, was the paradoxical result of a life that had exploded. An uncontrollable chaos was what crackled away below his silence and his immobility.

Langlais was not a doctor, and he had never saved anyone. But his own life had taught him the unpredictable therapeutic power of precision. It could be said that he treated himself with precision. It was the medicine that, dissolved in every sip of his life, kept the bane of bewilderment at bay. He thought that Adams's unassailable distance would have crumbled only under the patient daily drill of some precision. He felt that this should be, in some way, a *gentle* precision, only tinged with the coldness of a mechanical rite, and cultivated in the warmth of a little poetry. He searched for this for a long time in the world of things and gestures that had its home around him. And in the end he found it. And to those who, not without a certain sarcasm, dared ask him, "And what might be this prodigious medicine with which you think to save your savage?" He liked to reply, "My roses."

In the same way as a child might place a lost bird in the warmth of a nest made of cloth, Langlais placed Adams in his garden. An admirable garden, in which the most refined geometries kept the explosion of all the colors under control, and the discipline of rigid symmetries ruled the spectacular, closely ranked flowers and plants from all over the world. A garden in which the chaos of life became a divinely precise figure.

It was there that Adams slowly became himself again. For months he remained silent, only docilely allowing himself to be taught a thousand precise rules. Then his absence began to become a vague presence, punctuated here and there by brief phrases, and no longer tinged with the stubborn survival of the animal that had gone to ground within him. After a year, no one would have doubted, on seeing him, that he was the most classic and perfect of gardeners: silent and imperturbable, slow and precise in his gestures, inscrutable and ageless. The clement god of a miniature creation.

In all that time, Langlais never asked him anything. He exchanged few words with him, mostly to do with the state of health of the irises and the unpredictable changes in the weather. Neither of the two ever alluded to the past, to any past. He was waiting, was Langlais. He was not in a hurry. On the contrary, he was enjoying the pleasures of waiting. So much so that it was with an absurd touch of disappointment that, one day, while strolling in a secondary avenue of the garden where he happened to pass close to Adams, he saw him look up from a pearl-colored petunia and distinctly heard him pronounce—apparently to no one—these precise words:

"It has no walls, Timbuktu, because they have always thought, down there, that its beauty alone would stop any enemy."

Then Adams fell silent and looked down at the pearl-colored petunia once more. Langlais walked on, without saying a word, along the little avenue. Not even God, if he existed, would have noticed anything.

From that day, all of Adams's stories began to flow out of him. In the most diverse moments and according to inscrutable times and liturgies. Langlais limited himself to listening. He never asked a question. He listened and did no more. Sometimes they were mere phrases. Other times, authentic accounts. Adams narrated with a soft, warm voice. With surprising art, he measured words and silences. There was something hypnotic about the way he psalmodized fantastic images. To listen to him was spellbinding. And Langlais was enchanted.

Nothing of what he heard, in those tales, ended up in his tomes bound in dark leather. The Realm, in this case, did not come into it. Those stories were for him. He had waited until they bloomed from the womb of a violated, dead land. Now he was harvesting them. They were the refined gift he had decided to offer to his own solitude. He imagined himself growing old in the devoted shadow of those stories. And dying, one day, with his eyes full of the image, forbidden to any other white man, of the most beautiful garden in Timbuktu.

He thought that everything would always remain so magically light and easy. He could not foresee that he would soon relate that man named Adams to something surprisingly ferocious.

SOME TIME AFTER Adams's arrival, Admiral Langlais chanced to find himself burdened with the disagreeable and banal necessity of staking his life on a game of chess. Along with his little retinue, he was surprised in the open countryside by a bandit notorious in the area for his madness and the cruelty of his deeds. But in this case, surprisingly, he was inclined not to treat his victims with ferocity. He held only Langlais and sent back all the others to see to the task of raising the enormous sum required for the ransom. Langlais knew he was rich enough to buy back his freedom. What he could not foresee was whether the bandit would be patient enough to wait for all that money to arrive. For the first time in his life he felt the pungent odor of death upon him.

He spent two days blindfolded and shackled in a cart that rolled along unceasingly. On the third day they made him get out. When they took off his blindfold, he found himself seated in front of the bandit. Between the two men stood a small table. On the table, a chessboard. The bandit's explanation was laconic. He would give him one chance. One game. If he won, he would be freed. If he lost, he would be killed.

Langlais tried to make him see reason. As a corpse he was not worth a penny, why throw away a fortune like that?

69

"I didn't ask you what you thought about it. I asked you for a yes or a no. Make haste."

A maniac. This one was a maniac. Langlais realized he had no choice.

"As you wish," he said, and looked down at the chessboard. It was not long before he realized that the bandit's madness was of a brutally astute variety. Not only had he taken the white pieces—it would have been foolish to expect the contrary—but the man was playing with a second queen neatly ensconced in place of the king's bishop. A curious variation.

"A king," explained the bandit, indicating himself, "and two queens," he added mockingly, indicating the two women, beautiful indeed, who were seated beside him. This pleasantry unleashed unrestrained laughter and wholehearted yells of approval among the onlookers. Less amused, Langlais lowered his gaze, thinking that he was about to die in the stupidest manner possible.

The bandit's first move brought with it the return of absolute silence. King's pawn forward two squares. It was Langlais's turn. He hesitated for a few moments. It was as if he were waiting for something, but he did not know what it was. He understood only when, within his head, he heard a voice pronounce with magnificent calm, "Knight to the file of the king's bishop."

This time he did not look around. He knew that voice. And he knew that it was not there. God knows how, but it was coming from far away. He took the knight and placed it in front of the king's bishop's pawn.

By the sixth move he was one piece up. On the eighth, he

70

castled. By the eleventh he was the master of the middle board. Two moves later he sacrificed a bishop, which allowed him to take the first of the opposing queens in the next move. He trapped the second with a combination that—and he realized this—he would never have been capable of without the precise guidance of that absurd voice. As the resistance of the white pieces gradually crumbled, he sensed that the bandit's ferocious rage and bewilderment were growing. It got to the point where he was afraid to win. But the voice granted him no respite.

On the twenty-third move, the bandit virtually handed him a castle, following an error that was so obvious it seemed a surrender. Without thinking, Langlais was about to take advantage of this when the voice suggested peremptorily, "Watch out for the king, admiral."

Watch out for the king? Langlais stopped himself. The white king was sitting in an absolutely innocuous position, behind the remains of a hastily contrived castling move. Watch out for what? He stared at the chessboard without understanding.

"Watch out for the king."

The voice fell silent.

Everything fell silent.

A few moments.

Then Langlais understood. It was like a flash that crossed his mind a moment before the bandit produced a knife from nowhere and rapidly sought his heart with the blade. Langlais was faster. He blocked his arm, managed to wrest the knife from him, and, following through the movement he had begun, slashed the bandit's throat wide open.

The bandit crashed to the ground. Horrified, the two women ran away. All the others seemed petrified by amazement. Langlais kept calm. With a gesture that afterwards he would not have hesitated to judge uselessly solemn, he took the white king and tipped it over on the chessboard. Then he got up, clutching the knife tightly in his fist, and moved quickly away from the chessboard. Nobody moved. He mounted the first horse he came across. He cast a final glance at that strange scene out of popular theater and fled. As often happens in life's crucial moments, he found himself capable of a sole, absolutely insignificant thought: it was the first time— the first—that he had won with the black pieces.

WHEN HE GOT BACK to his palace, he found Adams stretched out in bed, unconscious and in the grip of a brain fever. The doctors did not know what to do. He said, "Do nothing. Nothing."

Four days later, Adams came to. There was Langlais, at his bedside. They looked at each other. Adams closed his eyes again. And Langlais said, in a low voice, "I owe you my life."

"*One* life," said Adams. Then he reopened his eyes and stared Langlais straight in the eye. It was not the look of a gardener, that glance. It was the look of an animal stalking its prey.

"My life means nothing to me. It is another life I want."

What that meant, Langlais was to understand much later, when it was too late to avoid hearing it.

A MOTIONLESS GARDENER, standing before an admiral's desk. Books and papers everywhere. But orderly. Orderly. And candelabras, carpets, the fragrance of leather, somber pictures, blackish curtains, maps, weapons, coins, portraits. Silverware. The admiral proffered a leaf of paper to the gardener and said,

"The Almayer Inn. A place by the sea, near Quartel."

"Is she there?"

"Yes."

The gardener folded the sheet of paper, put it in his pocket, and said, "I shall leave this evening."

The admiral lowered his gaze and, as he did so, heard the other's voice pronounce the word "Good-bye."

The gardener went toward the door. The admiral, without even looking at him, murmured, "And afterwards? What will happen afterwards?"

The gardener halted. "Nothing anymore."

And he went out.

The admiral said nothing.

... AS LANGLAIS WAS LETTING his mind escape along the route of a ship that had flown away, literally, in the waters of Malagar, and Adams was considering stopping in front of a rose of Borneo to observe an insect that was laboring to climb up one of its petals until the moment came when it gave up and flew away, in this sense similar to the ship that had obeyed the same instinct when sailing off Malagar, both of them comrades in their implicit refutation of the real and in the choice of that aerial flight, and united, in that instant, by their being images that had simultaneously alighted on the retina and the memory of two men whom nothing could have separated anymore and for whom those two flights, of the insect and the sailing ship, embodied their mutual dismay at the bitter taste of the end and the disconcerting discovery of how silent destiny is, when, suddenly, it explodes.

CHAPTER 8

ON THE FIRST FLOOR of the Almayer Inn, in a room that gave onto the hills, Elisewin was struggling with the night. Motionless, under the covers, she was waiting to discover which would be the first to come, sleep or fear.

The sound of the sea could be heard, like a continuous landslide, the incessant thunder of a storm that was the child of some unknown sky. It never stopped. It did not know weariness. Or mercy.

If you look at it, you don't notice how much noise it makes. But in the dark . . . All that infinity becomes only clamor, a wall of sound, a blind, tormenting howl. You cannot switch off the sea, when it burns in the night.

Elisewin felt a bubble of emptiness burst in her head. She knew well that secret explosion, that invisible, unspeakable anguish. But knowing it was useless. Useless. The insidious, slinking malaise—an obscene stepfather—was about to take her. It was come to take back its own.

It was not so much that cold that filtered through from inside her, and not even her wildly beating heart, or the cold sweat all over, or the trembling of her hands. The worst thing was that feeling of disappearing, of losing touch with one's mind, of being only vague panic and starts of fear. Thoughts like scraps of rebellion—shivers—her face set in a grimace, trying to keep her eyes closed—trying not to look at the dark, a horror with no escape. A war.

Elisewin managed to think of the door that, a few yards from her, connected her room with that of Father Pluche. A few yards. She had to make it. Now she would get up and without opening her eyes she would find it, and then all that was needed was Father Pluche's voice, even if it was only his voice, and it would all be over—all she had to do was get up from there, find the strength to take a few steps, cross the room, open the door—get up, slip out from under the covers, slip along the wall—get up, stand up, take those few steps—get up, keep the eyes closed, find that door, open it—get up, try to breathe, and then get away from the bed—get up, don't die—get up from there—get up. How horrible. How horrible.

It was not a few yards. It was miles, it was an eternity: the same distance that separated her from her real room, and her things, and her father, and her own place.

Everything was far away. Everything was lost.

Such wars cannot be won. And Elisewin surrendered.

As if dying, she opened her eyes.

She did not understand immediately.

She had not expected it.

The room was lit. A tiny light. But everywhere. Warm.

She turned. On a seat beside the bed was Dira, with a big book open on her knees, and a candle holder in her hand. The candle was burning. A little flame, in the dark that was no more.

Elisewin lay still, her head raised up a little from the pillow, looking. She seemed to be elsewhere, that little girl, and yet she was there. Her eyes fixed on those pages, her feet that did not even reach the floor and swung slowly back and forth: shoes on a swing, attached to two legs and a little skirt.

Elisewin let her head fall back on the pillow. She saw the candle flame smoking motionless. And the room around her slept sweetly. She felt tired, a wonderful tiredness. She just had time to think

"You can't hear the sea anymore."

Then she closed her eyes. And she fell asleep.

In the morning she found the candle holder, solitary, standing on the seat. The candle still burning. As if none of it had been consumed. As if it had kept vigil over a night only an instant long. An invisible flame against the great light that was bringing the new day through the window and into the room.

Elisewin got up. She blew out the candle. From all over arrived the strange music of a tireless musician. A huge sound. A spectacle.

The sea had returned.

PLASSON AND BARTLEBOOM went out together, that morning. Each with his own instruments: easel, paints, and brushes for Plasson, notebooks and various measuring devices for Bartleboom. You would have said that they had just cleared out a mad inventor's attic. One was wearing a fisherman's jacket and waders, and the other a set of professorial tails, a woolen hat on his head, and gloves without fingers, such as pianists use. Perhaps the inventor was not the only madman around there.

In reality, Plasson and Bartleboom did not even know each other. Their paths had crossed only a few times, in the corridors of the inn, or in the dining room. They would probably never have ended up there, on the beach, walking together toward their respective places of work, had Ann Deverià not decided it would be that way.

"It's amazing. If someone were to put you two together, he would obtain a single perfect lunatic. According to me, God is still up there, with the great puzzle under his nose, wondering what happened to those two pieces that fitted so well together."

"What's a puzzle?" asked Bartleboom at the same moment Plasson inquired, "What's a puzzle?"

The next morning they were walking on the seashore, each with his own instruments, but together, toward the paradoxical duties that constituted their daily labors.

Plasson had made money in the preceding years, by becoming the capital's best-loved portrait artist. You could say that in all the city there was no family genuinely greedy for money that did not have a Plasson in the house. Portraits, let it be well understood, only portraits. Landowners, sickly wives, bloated children, wrinkled great-aunts, rubicund industrialists, marriageable young ladies, ministers, priests, operatic prima donnas, military men, poetesses, violinists, academics, kept women, bankers, infant prodigies: from the walls of the capital's most genteel residences peeked, suitably framed, hundreds of astonished faces, inevitably ennobled by what in the salons was known as "the Plasson touch": a curious stylistic characteristic otherwise expressible in the skill, genuinely singular, with which the esteemed painter could bestow a glint of intelligence upon any gaze, no matter how bovine. "No matter how bovine" was the specification that was usually employed in the salons.

Plasson could have carried on like that for years. The faces of the rich are never-ending. But, out of the blue, one day he decided to drop everything. And to leave. A very precise idea, secretly nursed for years, carried him off.

To make a portrait of the sea.

He sold everything he possessed, abandoned his studio, and left for a journey that, as far he knew, might never end. There were thousands of miles of coastline, around the world. It was going to be no small matter, finding the right place.

When gossipmongers asked him the reason for that unusual desertion, he made no mention of the question of the sea. So they wanted to know what lay behind the retirement of the greatest master of the sublime art of portraiture. His response was a laconic phrase that subsequently lent itself unceasingly to a wide variety of interpretations:

"I am fed up with pornography."

Then he left. No one would find him anymore.

Bartleboom knew nothing about any of these things. He could not know them. That is why, there on the shore of the sea, having exhausted all small talk about the weather, he ventured to ask, just to keep the conversation going, "Have you been painting long?"

On that occasion, too, Plasson was laconic.

"Never done anything else."

Anyone listening to Plasson would have concluded that there were only two possibilities: either he was intolerably haughty or he was stupid. But there, too, you had to understand. One curious thing about Plasson was that when he talked, he never finished a sentence. He could not manage to finish one. He would arrive at the end only if the sentence did not exceed seven or eight words. If not, he would get lost halfway. For this reason, especially with strangers, he would try to limit himself to brief, succinct propositions. And it should be said that he was talented in this sense. Of course, this made him seem a little superior and irritatingly sententious. But it was always better than seeming vaguely doltish, which was what regularly happened when he launched into compound sentences or even only simple sentences, as he could never manage to finish them.

"Tell me, Plasson: Is there anything in the world that you manage to bring to a conclusion?" Ann Deverià had asked him one day, pinpointing the heart of the problem with her customary cynicism.

"Yes: disagreeable conversations," he had replied, getting up from the table and going off to his room. He had a flair, as has been said, for finding brief replies. Real flair.

Bartleboom did not know these things, either. He could not know them. But he was quick to understand them.

Under the midday sun, Plasson and he seated on the beach, eating the few things that Dira had prepared. The easel stuck in the sand, a few yards away. The usual white canvas, on the easel. The usual north wind, on everything.

BARTLEBOOM: Do you paint one of these pictures a day?

PLASSON: In a certain sense . . .

BARTLEBOOM: Your room must be full of them . . .

PLASSON: No, I throw them away.

BARTLEBOOM: Away?

PLASSON: You see that one there, on the easel?

BARTLEBOOM: Yes.

PLASSON: They are all like that, more or less.

BARTLEBOOM: . . .

PLASSON: Would you keep them?

A cloud obscures the sun. The sudden cold catches you by surprise. Bartleboom puts his woolen hat on again.

PLASSON: It's difficult.

BARTLEBOOM: You don't have to tell me that. I couldn't

even draw this piece of cheese, it's a mystery how you manage to do those things, it's a mystery to me.

PLASSON: The *sea* is difficult.

BARTLEBOOM: ...

PLASSON: It's difficult to know where to begin. You see, when I used to do portraits, portraits of people, I used to know where to begin, I would look at those faces and I knew exactly (stop)

BARTLEBOOM: ...

PLASSON: ...

BARTLEBOOM: ...

PLASSON: ...

BARTLEBOOM: You used to paint people's portraits?

PLASSON: Yes.

BARTLEBOOM: My goodness, I've wanted to have my portrait painted for years now, really, now you will think this stupid, but ...

PLASSON: When I painted people's portraits, I used to begin with the eyes. I would forget all the rest and concentrate on the eyes, I would study them, for minutes and minutes, then I sketched them in, with a pencil, and that was the secret, because once you have drawn the eyes (stop)

BARTLEBOOM: ...

PLASSON: ...

BARTLEBOOM: What happens once you have drawn the eyes?

PLASSON: It happens that all the rest just follows, it's as if all the other pieces slip into place around that initial point by themselves, there's not even any need to (stop)

BARTLEBOOM: . . . There's not even any need.

PLASSON: No. One can almost avoid looking at the sitter, everything comes by itself, the mouth, the curve of the neck, even the hands . . . But the fundamental thing is to start from the eyes, do you see, and this is where the real problem lies, the problem that drives me mad, lies exactly here (stop)

BARTLEBOOM: . . .

PLASSON: . . .

BARTLEBOOM: Do you have an idea where the problem lies, Plasson?

Agreed: it was a little contrived. But it worked. It was only a question of getting him under way again. Every time. With patience. Bartleboom, as can be deduced from his singular love life, was a patient man.

PLASSON: The problem is, *where the dickens are the eyes of the sea?* I shall never get anything done until I find out, because that is the *beginning*, do you see? The beginning of everything, and until I know where they are, I shall carry on spending my days looking at this damned stretch of water without (stop)

BARTLEBOOM: . . .

PLASSON: . . .

Bartleboom: . . .

Plasson: This is the problem, Bartleboom . . .

Magic: this time he got started again on his own.

Plasson: This is the problem: *Where does the sea begin?*

Bartleboom said nothing.

The sun came and went, between one cloud and the next. It was the north wind, as usual, which organized the silent spectacle. The sea carried on imperturbably reciting its psalms. If it had eyes, it was not looking in that direction at that moment.

Silence.

Minutes of silence.

Then Plasson turned to Bartleboom and said, all in one breath, "And you, sir, what are you studying with all those funny instruments of yours?"

Bartleboom smiled.

"Where the sea *ends*."

Two pieces of a puzzle. Made for each other. In some part of the heavens, an old Gentleman, in that moment, had finally found them again.

"What the devil? . . . I *said* that they couldn't have disappeared."

· · ·

"THE ROOM IS on the ground floor. Down that way, the third door on the left. There are no keys. No one has them here. You ought to write your name in that book. It's not obligatory, but everybody does it here."

The register with the signatures waited open on a wooden bookrest. A freshly made bed of paper that awaited the dreams of other people's names. The man's pen barely brushed it.

Adams.

Then he hesitated a moment, motionless.

"If you want to know the names of the others, you can ask me. It's hardly a secret."

Adams looked up from the register and smiled.

"It's a nice name: Dira."

The little girl was stunned. She instinctively shot a glance at the register.

"My name isn't written there."

"Not there."

It was already hard to believe she was ten, that little girl. But when she wanted, she could seem a thousand years older. She fixed Adams smack-dab in the eye, and what she said, she said with a cutting voice that seemed to belong to a woman who, wherever she was, was not there.

"Adams is not your real name."

"No?"

"No."

"And how do you know?"

"I can read too."

Adams smiled. He bent over, took his luggage, and went off toward his room.

"The third door on the left," yelled a voice from behind him that was once more that of a little girl.

There were no keys. He opened the door and went in. It was not that he expected much. But at least he expected to find the room empty.

"Oh, excuse me," said Father Pluche, moving away from the window and instinctively adjusting his cassock.

"Have I got the wrong room?"

"No, no . . . it is I who . . . you see, I have the room above, but it gives onto the hills, you cannot see the sea: I chose it out of prudence."

"Prudence?"

"Forget it, it's a long story . . . The fact is, I wanted to see the view from here, but now I must be off, I should never have come, had I known . . ."

"You may stay, if you wish."

"No, I will go now. You must have lots to do, have you just arrived?"

Adams put his luggage on the floor.

"How stupid, of course you have just arrived . . . well, I'm off, then. Oh . . . my name is Pluche, Father Pluche."

Adams nodded. "Father Pluche."

"Yes."

"Good-bye, Father Pluche."

"Yes, good-bye."

He slipped toward the door and went out. On passing by the reception desk—if we want to call it that—he felt obliged to mutter, "I didn't know that someone would have come, I only wanted to see how the sea looked . . ."

"It doesn't matter, Father Pluche."

He was about to go out, when he stopped, turned and retraced his steps, and, leaning slightly over the desk, asked Dira *sotto voce*, "According to you, might he be a doctor?"

"Who?"

"Him."

"Ask him."

"He doesn't strike me as one who is dying to hear questions. He didn't even tell me his name."

Dira hesitated a second.

"Adams."

"Adams, that's all?"

"Adams, that's all."

"Oh."

He would have gone, but he still had something to say. He said it in an even lower voice.

"His eyes . . . . he has eyes like those of an animal stalking its prey."

This time he had really finished.

ANN DEVERIÀ WALKING along the shore, in her purple cloak. Beside her, a little girl called Elisewin, with her little white umbrella. She is sixteen. Perhaps she will die, perhaps she will live. Who knows. Ann Deverià speaks without taking her eyes off what lies before her. *Before* in many senses.

"My father did not want to die. He was getting old, but he would not die. Diseases were devouring him and he, undaunted, clung on to life. In the end he did not even leave his room anymore. They had to do everything for him. Years like that. He was barricaded behind a kind of stronghold, all his, built in the most invisible corner of himself. He gave up everything, but he clung on ferociously to the only two things that really meant something to him: writing and hating. He wrote with difficulty, with the hand that he could still manage to move. And hated with his eyes. As for talking, he did not talk anymore, right until the end. He would write and he would hate. When he died—because finally he died—my mother took all those hundreds of scribbled sheets and read them, one by one. There were the names of all those he had known, one after another. And next to each one there was a minute description of a horrible death. I have not read those sheets. But those eyes—those eyes that hated, every minute of every day, right until the end—I had seen them. And how I had seen them. I married my husband because he had kind eyes. It was the only thing that mattered to me. He had kind eyes.

"Besides, it is not as if life goes as you think it does. Life follows its path. And you follow yours. And it is not the same path. And so . . . It is not that I wanted to be happy, no. I wanted . . . to save myself, that's all: to save myself. But I understood late the path one should follow: the path of the desires. One expects other things to save people. Duty, honesty, being good, being just. No. It is the desires that save. They are the only real thing. You stick with them, and you will save yourself. But I found this out too late. If you give life the time, it will turn things around in a strange, inexorable way: and at that point you realize that you cannot desire something without hurting yourself. That's where everything falls apart, there's no way out, the more you struggle, the more tangled the net becomes, the more you rebel, the more you hurt yourself. There's no escape. When it was too late, I began to desire. With all the strength I possessed. You cannot imagine how very badly I hurt myself.

"Do you know what is beautiful here? Look: we walk, we leave all those footprints on the sand, and they stay there, precise, ordered. But tomorrow you will get up, you will look at this enormous beach and nothing will remain, not a footprint, not a sign, nothing. The sea rubs things out during the night. The tide conceals. It is as if no one had ever passed by here. It is as if we had never existed. If there is, in the world, a place where you can fancy yourself nothing-ness, that place is here. It is land no longer, it is not yet sea. It's not sham life, it's not real life.

"It's *time*. Time that passes. That's all.

"It would make a splendid refuge. We would be invisible to any enemy. Suspended. White like Plasson's pictures. Imperceptible even to ourselves. But there is something that undermines this purgatory. And it is something from which there is no escape. The sea. The sea enchants, the sea kills, it moves, it frightens, it also makes you laugh sometimes, it disappears every now and then, it disguises itself as a lake, or it constructs tempests, devours ships, gives away riches, it gives no answers, it is wise, it is gentle, it is powerful, it is unpredictable. But, above all, the sea calls. You will discover this, Elisewin. All it does, basically, is this: it *calls.* It never stops, it gets under your skin, it is upon you, it is you it wants. You can even pretend to ignore it, but it's no use. It will still call you. This sea you are looking at and all the others that you will not see, but will always be there, lying patiently in wait for you, one step beyond your life. You will hear them calling, tirelessly. It happens in this purgatory of sand. It would happen in any paradise, and in any inferno. Without explaining anything, without telling you where, there will always be a sea, which will call you."

Ann Deverià stops. She bends over and takes her shoes off. She leaves them on the sand. She starts walking again, barefoot. Elisewin does not move. She waits until she has moved a few steps farther away. Then she says, in a voice loud enough to be heard, "In a few days I shall be leaving here. And I shall go into the sea. And I shall get better. This is what I want. To get better. To live. And, one day, to become beautiful like you."

Ann Deverià turns. She smiles. She searches for words. She finds them.

"Will you take me with you?"

THIS TIME there are two people seated on Bartleboom's windowsill. The usual little boy. And Bartleboom. Their legs dangling over the emptiness below. Their gaze dangling over the sea.

"Listen, Dood . . ."

The little boy's name was Dood.

"Given that you are always here . . ."

"Mmmmh . . ."

"Perhaps you know."

"What?"

"Where does the sea have its eyes?"

". . ."

"Because it does have them, doesn't it?"

"Yes."

"And where the dickens are they?"

"The ships."

"The ships *what*?"

"The ships are the eyes of the sea."

Bartleboom was flabbergasted. He really had not thought of that.

"But there are hundreds of ships . . ."

"The sea has hundreds of eyes. You can hardly expect it to get things done with only two . . ."

Quite. With all the work it has to do. And as big as it is. There is good sense in all this.

"Yes, but then, excuse me . . ."

"Mmmm."

"And people who are shipwrecked? The storms, the typhoons, all that stuff there . . . Why ever should it swallow all those ships, if they are its eyes?"

Dood looks almost a little out of patience, when he turns toward Bartleboom and says, "But you, . . . don't you ever close your eyes?"

Christ. He has an answer for everything, this boy.

He thinks, does Bartleboom. He thinks and mulls things over and reflects and reasons. Then he suddenly jumps down from the windowsill. Toward the room, of course. You would need wings to jump down in the other direction.

"Plasson . . . I must find Plasson . . . I have to tell him . . . blast, it wasn't so difficult, all you had to do was think about it a little . . ."

He searches feverishly for his woolen hat. He does not find it. Wholly understandable: it is on his head. He desists. He runs out of the room.

"See you later, Dood."

"See you later."

The boy remains there, with his eyes fixed on the sea. He stays there for a little. Then he takes a good look to see that no one is around and suddenly jumps down from the windowsill. Toward the beach, of course.

ONE DAY they woke up and nothing was there anymore. It was not just the footprints on the sand that had disappeared. Everything had disappeared. So to speak.

Unbelievable fog.

"It is not fog, only clouds."

Unbelievable clouds.

"They are sea clouds. Sky clouds stay up above. Sea clouds stay down low. They come only seldom. Then they go."

Dira knew loads of things.

Certainly if you looked outside it was rather a shock. Only the previous evening the sky had been full of stars, fabulous. And now it was like being inside a cup of milk. Not to mention the cold. Like being inside a cup of cold milk.

"It's the same in Carewall."

Father Pluche was standing there with his nose pressed against the windows, enthralled.

"It lasts days and days. It doesn't move an inch. There it's fog. Decidedly fog. And when it comes you can't make head or tail of anything anymore. Even in the daytime people walk around with a torch in hand. Trying to work things out. Not even that is much help, however. But at night you really don't know what's happening at all. Just think, Arlo Crut went home one evening, but he got the wrong house and wound up in the bed of Metel Crut, his brother. Metel didn't even notice, he was sleeping like a log, but his wife certainly noticed. A man had slipped into her bed. Unbelievable. Well, do you know what she said?"

And here, in Father Pluche's head, the usual gauntlet was thrown down. Two fine phrases left the starting blocks in his brain with a well-defined finishing line ahead of them: that of finding a voice with which to come out into the open. The most sensible of the two, considering that this was still the voice of a priest, was certainly "Do it, and I'll start screaming."

But this phrase was flawed by the fact that it was false. The other one, the true one, prevailed.

"Do it, or I'll start screaming."

"Father Pluche!"

"What did I say?"

"What did you say?"

"Did *I* say something?"

They were all in the big room that gave onto the sea, sheltered from that inundation of clouds, but not from the disagreeable sensation of not quite knowing what to do. Doing nothing is one thing. Being unable to do anything is another. It's different.

They were all a bit bewildered. Fish in an aquarium. The most restless of all was Plasson: in waders and fisherman's jacket, he was wandering about nervously observing the sea of milk on the other side of the windows, a sea that didn't move an inch.

"It really does resemble one of your pictures," noted Ann Deverià out loud from the depths of a wicker armchair whence she too was observing the great spectacle. Everything wonderfully white.

Plasson carried on pacing backward and forward. As if he had not even heard.

Bartleboom looked up from the book he was idly leafing through.

"You are too severe, Madame Deverià. Mr. Plasson is trying to do something very difficult. And his pictures are no whiter than the pages of this book of mine."

"Are you writing a book?" asked Elisewin from her seat, in front of the large fireplace.

"A sort of book."

"Did you hear, Father Pluche? Mr. Bartleboom writes books."

"No, it's not exactly a book . . ."

"It is an encyclopedia," explained Ann Deverià.

"An encyclopedia?"

And they were off. Sometimes it takes nothing to forget the great sea of milk, even as it continues screwing you up. Perhaps all you need is the harsh sound of a strange word. *Encyclopedia*. A single word. And they were off. All of them: Bartleboom, Elisewin, Father Pluche, Plasson. And Madame Deverià.

"Bartleboom, don't be modest, tell the young lady that story of the limits, the rivers and all the rest."

"It is called the *Encyclopedia of the Limits to be found in Nature* . . ."

"A fine title. I had a teacher, at the seminary . . ."

"Let him talk, Father Pluche . . ."

"I have been working on it for twelve years. It is a complicated business . . . to all practical purposes I study the point at which Nature arrives, or, better, where it decides to stop. Because it always stops, sooner or later. This is scientific. For example . . ."

"Give the example of the copironus."

"Well, that was a rather particular case."

"Have you already heard the story of the copironi, Plasson?"

"Look, he told me the story of the copironi, my dear Madame Deverià, and you had it from me."

"My goodness, that was a very long sentence, my compliments, Plasson, you are improving."

"Well then, these copironi?"

"The copironi live on the northern glaciers. They are perfect animals in their way. They practically do not grow old. If they wished, they could live for eternity."

"Horrible."

"But be careful, Nature controls everything, nothing escapes her. And so here is what happens: at a certain point, when it is around seventy, eighty years old, the copironus stops eating."

"No."

"Yes. They stop eating. On the average they live another three years, in that state. Then they die."

"Three years without eating?"

"On the average. Some resist for even longer. But in the end, and this is important, they die. It's a scientific fact."

"But it's suicide!"

"In a certain sense."

"And according to you, we should believe you, Bartleboom?"

"Look here, I also have a drawing . . . A drawing of a copironus . . ."

"My goodness, you're right, Bartleboom, you really do draw badly, really, I have never seen a drawing—"

"I didn't make it . . . it was the sailor who told me the story that drew it . . ."

"A sailor?"

"You had all this story from a sailor?"

"Yes, why?"

"Oh, well done, Bartleboom, really scientific . . ."

"I believe you."

"Thank you, Miss Elisewin."

"I believe you, and so does Father Pluche, don't you?"

"Certainly . . . it's a very likely story, in fact, if I remember well, I have heard it before, it must have been at the seminary . . ."

"One really learns loads of things in these seminaries . . . are there any for ladies?"

"Now that I think of it, Plasson, you could make me the illustrations for the Encyclopedia, it would be splendid, would it not?"

"Would I have to draw the copironus?"

"Well, let's forget about the copironus, but there are loads of other things . . . I have written eight hundred seventy-two entries, you could choose the ones you prefer . . ."

"Eight hundred seventy-two?"

"Doesn't it strike you as a good idea, Madame Deverià?"

"For the entry sea, I should perhaps do without the illustration . . ."

"Father Pluche draws the pictures for his book himself."

"Elisewin, never mind . . ."

"But it's true . . ."

"Don't tell me we have another scientist . . ."

"It's a very beautiful book."

"Do you really write, too, Father Pluche?"

97

"Not really, it is a rather . . . particular thing, it's not exactly what you would call a book."

"Yes, it is a book."

"Elisewin . . ."

"He never lets anyone see it, but it's very beautiful."

"I say it is poetry."

"Not exactly."

"But you were close."

"Songs?"

"No."

"Come, Father Pluche, must we pray you?"

"That's it, in fact . . ."

"In fact what?"

"No, I mean, apropos of prayer . . ."

"Don't tell me that . . ."

"Prayers, they are prayers."

"Prayers?"

"Adieu . . ."

"But they are not like the others, Father Pluche's prayers . . ."

"I find it an excellent idea. I have always felt the lack of a good prayer book."

"Bartleboom, a scientist should not *pray*, if he is a real scientist he should not even think of—"

"On the contrary! Precisely because we study nature, nature being none other than the mirror . . ."

"He also wrote a very fine one about a doctor. A doctor is a scientist, isn't that so?"

"How do you mean *about* a doctor?"

"It is entitled *Prayer for a Doctor Who Saves an Invalid and at the Instant in Which the Latter Gets Up, Cured, the Former Feels Infinitely Tired.*"

"What?"

"But that's no title for a prayer."

"I told you that Father Pluche's prayers are not like the others."

"But do they all have titles like that?"

"Well, I made some titles a bit shorter, but that's the idea."

"Tell us some others, Father Pluche . . ."

"Oh, so now you are interested in prayers, eh, Plasson?"

"I don't know . . . there is the *Prayer for a Little Boy Who Cannot Say the Letter R*, or the *Prayer of a Man Who Is Falling into a Ravine and Doesn't Want to Die* . . ."

"I don't believe it . . ."

"Well, obviously it is very short, a few words only . . . then there is the *Prayer of an Old Man Whose Hands Shake*, things like that."

"Extraordinary!"

"And how many have you written?"

"A few . . . they are not easy to write, every so often one feels like it, but if inspiration will not come . . ."

"But roughly how many?"

"For the present . . . nine thousand five hundred and two."

"No . . ."

"Fantastic . . ."

"Good heavens, Bartleboom, your encyclopedia is a little notebook in comparison."

"But how do you do it, Father Pluche?"

"I don't know."

"Yesterday he wrote a very beautiful one."

"Elisewin . . ."

"Really."

"Elisewin, please . . ."

"Yesterday evening he wrote one about you, sir."

Suddenly everybody fell silent.

Yesterday evening he wrote one about you, sir.

But she did not say it looking at one of them.

Yesterday evening he wrote one about you, sir.

She was looking elsewhere when she said it, and it was there that everybody turned, taken by surprise.

A table, alongside the glass door at the entrance. A man seated at the table, a spent pipe in his hand. Adams. Nobody knows when he arrived there. Perhaps he has been there for a moment, perhaps he has always been there.

"Yesterday evening he wrote one about you, sir."

Everyone remained motionless. But Elisewin got up and went over to him.

"It is called the *Prayer for a Man Who Does Not Want to Say His Name.*"

But gently. She said it gently.

"Father Pluche thinks you are a doctor."

Adams smiles.

"Only now and then."

"But I say that you are a mariner."

All silent, the others. Motionless. But they did not miss a word, not one.

"Only now and then."

"And here, today, what are you?"

Adams shakes his head.

"Just somebody who is waiting."

Elisewin is standing in front of him. She has a precise and very simple question in mind:

"*What* are you waiting for?"

Only five words. But she cannot say them because a second before she does, she hears a voice murmur in her head, "Don't ask me, Elisewin. Don't ask me, I beg you."

She stands there motionless, without saying anything, her eyes fixed on those of Adams, which are as silent as stones.

Silence.

Then Adams looks up above her head and says, "What wonderful sunshine today."

On the other side of the windows, without a groan, every cloud has died, and the clear air of a day resuscitated from nothing breaks out with blinding force.

BEACH. And sea.

Light.

The north wind.

The silence of the tides.

Days. Nights.

A liturgy. Motionless, come to think of it. *Motionless.*

People like the gestures of a ritual.

Something other than *men.*

Gestures.

The breath of the evanescent daily ceremony, they are transformed into oxygen to form an angelic *surplace*.

Metabolized by the perfect landscape of the seashore, they are converted into figures like those on a silk fan.

More immutable with every day.

Placed within a stone's throw of the sea, their becoming is their passing away, and in the interstices of an elegant nothingness they receive the solace of a temporary nonexistence.

On that trompe-l'oeil of the soul there floats the argentine tinkle of their words, the only perceivable ripple on the still surface of the ineffable enchantment.

"DO YOU THINK I am mad?"

"No."

Bartleboom has told her the whole story. The letters, the mahogany box, the woman who waits. Everything.

"I have never told this to anyone before."

Silence. Evening. Ann Deverià. Her hair down. A long white nightgown hanging to her feet. Her room. The light flickering on the walls.

"Why me, Bartleboom?"

The Professor is mangling the hem of his jacket. It is not easy. Not easy at all.

"Because I need you to help me."

"Me?"

"You."

A man weaves great stories, that's a fact, and can go on for years believing in them; it does not matter how insane they are, and improbable, he carries them around, that's all. You can even be happy, with things like that. *Happy.* And it might never end. Then, one day, something snaps in the heart of the great fantastic contrivance, and all of a sudden, for no reason, it breaks without warning and you are left standing there, unable to understand how it is that that fabulous story is no longer with you, but *ahead* of you, as if it were another person's folly, and you are that other person. All of a sudden. Sometimes it takes a mere nothing. Perhaps only the emergence of a question. That can be enough.

"Madame Deverià . . . how shall I be able to recognize her, that woman, *my* woman, when I meet her?"

Perhaps only an elementary question that emerges from the subterranean lair in which it was buried. That can be enough.

"How shall I recognize her, when I meet her?"

Quite.

"But in all these years, have you never asked yourself this?"

"No. I knew that I would recognize her, that's all. But now I am afraid. I am afraid that I shall not realize. And she will move on. And I shall lose her."

He was really burdened by a world of anguish, was Professor Bartleboom.

"Teach me, Madame Deverià, how I shall recognize her, when I see her."

Elisewin was sleeping by the light of a candle and a little girl. And Father Pluche, among his prayers, and Plasson, in the whiteness of his pictures. Perhaps even Adams, the animal stalking its prey, was sleeping. The Almayer Inn was sleeping, rocked by the ocean sea.

"Close your eyes, Bartleboom, and give me your hands."

Bartleboom obeys. And instantly he feels that woman's face under his hands, and her lips as they play with his fingers, and then the slim neck and the nightgown opening, her hands guiding his along that warm and very soft skin, and they clutch them to her, to feel the secrets of that unknown body, to clutch that warmth, before drawing them back up to her shoulders, among her hair and once more between her lips, where his fingers slip back and forth until a voice comes to stop them and write in the silence:

"Look at me, Bartleboom."

The bodice of her nightgown has slipped down to her lap. Her eyes smile with no embarrassment.

"One day you will see a woman and feel all this without even touching her. Give your letters to her. You wrote them for her."

A thousand things are buzzing around Bartleboom's head while he withdraws his hands, holding them open, as if closing them might cause all to escape.

He was so confused when he left the room that he thought he saw, in the half-light, the unreal figure of a most beautiful little girl, hugging a large pillow, at the foot of the bed. With no clothes on. Her skin white as a sea cloud.

"WHEN DO YOU want to leave, Elisewin?" says Father Pluche.

"And you?"

"I don't want anything. But we must go to Daschenbach, sooner or later. It is there that you must take the cure. This . . . this is not a good place to get better."

"Why do you say so?"

"There is something . . . something *unhealthy* about this place. Haven't you noticed? That painter's white pictures, Professor Bartleboom's endless measurements . . . and then that lady who is so very beautiful and yet alone and unhappy, I don't know . . . not to mention that man who *waits* . . . what he does is wait. God knows for what, or whom . . . Everything has stopped one step short of things. There is nothing *real*, do you understand this?"

Elisewin kept silent and thought.

"And that's not all. Do you know what I have discovered? There is another guest in the inn. In the seventh room, the one that seems empty. Well, it's not empty. There is a man in there. But he never comes out. Dira did not want to tell me who he is. None of the others has ever seen him. They take his food to his room. Does that seem normal to you?"

Elisewin said nothing.

"What kind of place is this, where there are people who are invisible, or they go backward and forward ad infinitum, as if they had an eternity before them to . . ."

"This is the seashore, Father Pluche. Neither land nor sea. It's a place that does not exist."

Elisewin gets up, she smiles.

"It's a world of angels."

She is about to go out. She stops.

"We shall leave, Father Pluche. A few more days and we shall leave."

"So LISTEN CAREFULLY, Dol. You must watch the sea. And when you see a ship, you tell me. Understood?"

"Yes, Monsieur Plasson."

"Good lad."

The fact is that Plasson's eyesight is not up to much. He can see close up, but not things at a distance. He says that he has spent too much time looking at rich people's faces. It ruins the sight. Not to mention everything else. And so he looks for ships, but he cannot find them. Perhaps Dol will succeed.

"It's because the ships pass by far out, Mr. Plasson."

"Why?"

"They are afraid of the devil's footsteps."

"That is?"

"Rocks. There are rocks off the entire coast around here. They are close to the surface, but you can't always see them, by any means. So the ships stay well out to sea."

"All we needed was rocks."

"The devil put them there."

"Yes, Dol."

"Really! You see, the devil used to live down there, on Taby Island. Well, one day a little girl who was a saint took a boat and after rowing for three days and three nights she arrived at the island. Very beautiful."

"The island or the saint?"

"The little girl."

"Ah."

"She was so beautiful that when the devil saw her he was scared to death. He tried to chase her away, but she didn't budge. She just stayed there looking at him. Until one day the devil really couldn't stood it any longer . . ."

"Couldn't *stand* it."

"Couldn't stand it any longer and, howling, he ran and ran, into the sea, until he disappeared and no one ever saw him again."

"And the rocks, where do they come in?"

"They come in because for every step that the devil made as he ran away, a rock came out of the sea. Everywhere he set foot—bingo!—up popped a rock. And they're still there today. They are the devil's footsteps."

"A good story."

"Yes."

"Can you see anything?"

"No."

Silence.

"Are we going to stay here all day?"

"Yes."

Silence.

"I liked it better when I used to come for you in the evening with the boat."

"Keep your mind on the job, Dol."

"You could write a poem for them, Father Pluche."

"Are you saying that seagulls pray?"

"Certainly. Especially when they are about to die."

"And do you never pray, Bartleboom?"

Bartleboom adjusted the woolen hat on his head.

"I used to pray, once. Then I made a calculation. In eight years I had taken the liberty of asking the Almighty for two things. Result: my sister died and I have still to meet the woman I shall marry. Now I pray much less."

"I do not think that . . ."

"Numbers speak clearly, Father Pluche. The rest is poetry."

"Quite. If only we were a little more . . ."

"Don't make things difficult, Father Pluche. The question is a simple one. Do you really believe that God exists?"

"Well, now, *exists* strikes me as a slightly excessive term, but I believe he is there, that's it, in a world all of his own, *he is there.*"

"And what difference does it make?"

"It makes a difference, all right, Bartleboom, and how. Take for example this story of the seventh room . . . yes, the story of that man at the inn who never leaves his room, and all that."

"So?"

"No one has ever seen him. He eats, it would seem. But it could easily be a trick. He might not exist. Made up by Dira. But for us, in any case, *he would be there.* In the evening the lights are lit in that room, every so often sounds are heard, you yourself, I have seen you slow down when you pass that room, you try to see, to hear something . . . For us that man *is there.*"

"But it's not true, and then again he's mad, that one, he's a . . ."

"He's not mad, Bartleboom. Dira says he is a gentleman, a real gentleman. She says he has a secret, that's all, but he is a completely normal person."

"And you believe that?"

"I don't know who he is, I don't know if he *exists*, but I know that he's there. For me he's there. And he is a frightened man."

"Frightened?"

Bartleboom shakes his head.

"Frightened of what?"

"DON'T YOU GO down to the beach?"

"No."

"You don't take a walk, you don't write, you don't make pictures, you don't talk, you don't ask questions. You are waiting, aren't you?"

"Yes."

"Why? Why don't you do what you have to do, and get it over with?"

Adams looks up at that little girl who speaks with a woman's voice when she wants to, and at that moment she wants to.

"I have seen inns like this one in a thousand different parts of the world. Or perhaps I have seen this inn in a thousand different parts of the world. The same solitude, the same colors, the same fragrances, the same silence. People come here and time stops. For some it must be a feeling akin to happiness, don't you think?"

"For some."

"If I could turn back, then I would choose this: to live *in front of* the sea."

Silence.

"In front of it."

Silence.

"Adams . . ."

Silence.

"Stop waiting. It's not so difficult to kill someone."

"BUT ACCORDING TO YOU, shall I die, down there?"

"In Daschenbach?"

"When they put me in the sea."

"Come on . . ."

"You come on, tell me the truth, Father Pluche, don't joke."

"You will not die, I swear it to you, you will not die."

"And how do you know?"

"I know."

"Oof."

"I dreamed it."

"Dreamed it . . ."

"Listen to me, then. One evening I go off to sleep, I slip into bed, and when I am about to switch off the light, I see the door open and a little boy comes in. I thought he was a porter, something like that. And instead he comes up to me and says, 'Is there anything you want to dream of tonight, Father Pluche?' Just like that. And I say, 'The countess Varmeer having a bath.'"

"Father Pluche . . ."

"It was a joke, wasn't it? Well, he says nothing, smiles a bit, and off he goes. I fall asleep and what do I dream of?"

"The countess Varmeer having a bath."

"That's it."

"And how was she?"

"Oh, nothing, a disappointment . . ."

"Ugly?"

"She only *looks* slim, a disappointment . . . However . . . He returns every evening, that little boy. His name is Ditz. And each time he asks me if I want to dream of something. And so the day before yesterday I said to him, 'I want to dream of Élisewin. I want to dream of her as a grownup.' I fell asleep, and I dreamed of you."

"And how was I?"

"*Alive.*"

"Alive? And then what?"

"Alive. Don't ask me anything else. You were alive."

"Alive . . . me?"

ANN DEVERIÀ AND BARTLEBOOM, seated beside each other, in a beached boat.

"And what answer did you give him?" asked Bartleboom.

"I gave him no answer."

"No?"

"No."

"And what will happen now?"

"I don't know. I think he will come."

"Are you happy about that?"

"I want him. But I don't know."

"Perhaps he will come here and take you away, forever."

"Don't talk nonsense, Bartleboom."

"And why not? He loves you, you said so yourself, you are all he has in life . . ."

Ann Deverià's lover has finally discovered where her husband has confined her. He has written to her. In this moment he is perhaps already on his way toward that sea and that beach.

"I would come here and I would take you away, forever."

Ann Deverià smiles.

"Tell me again, Bartleboom. With exactly that tone of voice, I pray you. Tell me again."

"DOWN THERE . . . there it is, down there!"

"Down there, where?"

"There . . . no, farther to the right, that's it, there . . ."

"I see it! I see it, by God."

"Three masts!"

"Three masts?"

"It's a three-master, can't you see?"

"Three?"

"PLASSON, how long have we all been here?"

"Since time immemorial, Madame."

"No. Really."

"Since time immemorial, Madame. Really."

"ACCORDING TO ME, he's a gardener."

"Why?"

"He knows the names of the trees."

"And how do you know that, Elisewin?"

"I DON'T LIKE this business of the seventh room one little bit."

"What's it to you?"

"A man who will not show himself, it scares me."

"Father Pluche says that he's the one who is afraid."

"Afraid of what?"

"EVERY SO OFTEN I wonder what on earth we are waiting for."

Silence.

"For it to be too late, Madame."

THEY COULD HAVE gone on like that forever.

BOOK II

The Womb of the Sea

FOURTEEN DAYS AFTER setting sail from Rochefort, owing to the captain's incapacity and inaccurate
charts, the French naval frigate *Alliance* ran aground on a
sandbar, off the coast of Senegal. All attempts to free the hull
were vain. There was nothing else to do but abandon ship.
Since the longboats available were insufficient to accommo-
date the entire complement, a raft measuring about forty feet
in length and half that in width was constructed and lowered
onto the water. Onto it went 147 men: soldiers, sailors, a few
passengers, four officers, a doctor, and an engineer cartographer. The evacuation plan called for the four longboats to tow
the raft to the shore. Shortly after abandoning the wreck of
the *Alliance*, however, panic and confusion gripped the convoy

that was slowly trying to reach the coast. Out of baseness or ineptitude—no one ever managed to establish the truth—the longboats lost contact with the raft. The towing hawser snapped. Or someone cut it. The longboats continued toward land and the raft was abandoned to fend for itself. Not even half an hour later, dragged along by the current, it had already disappeared over the horizon.

FIRST is my name, Savigny.

First is my name, second is the gaze of those who abandoned us—their eyes, in that moment—fixed on the raft, they were unable to look elsewhere, but there was nothing behind that gaze, absolutely nothing, neither hate nor pity, remorse, fear, nothing. Their eyes.

First is my name, second those eyes, third a thought: I am going to die, I shall not die. I am going to die I shall not die I am going to die I shall not die I am—the water is up to our knees, the raft slips under the surface of the sea, weighed down by the burden of too many men—going to die I shall not die I am going to die I shall not die—the smell, the smell of fear, of sea and bodies, the wood creaking underfoot, the voices, the ropes to hang on to, my clothes, my weapons, the face of the man who—I am going to die I shall not die I am going to die I shall not die I am going to die—the waves all around, don't think, where is the land? who is taking us there, who is in command? the wind, the current, the prayers like groans, the prayers of rage, the howling of the sea, the fear that

First is my name, sec-
ond those eyes, third a thought and fourth the night to come,
clouds against the light of the moon, horrendous dark, only
sounds: shouts and groans and prayers and curses, and the sea
that is getting up and beginning to sweep that tangle of bodies
from every angle—there's nothing for it but to hang on to
what you can, a rope, the beams, someone's arm, all night long,
in the water, under the water, if only there were a light, any
kind of light, this darkness is eternal and the wailing that
accompanies every instant is intolerable—but one moment
I remember, under the slap of an unexpected wave, a wall
of water, I remember, suddenly, the silence, a blood-chilling
silence, an instant, and my screaming, my screaming, my
screaming,

First is my name, second those eyes, third a thought,
fourth the night to come, fifth the mangled bodies, trapped
between the boards of the raft, a man like a rag, hanging from
a post that had staved in his chest to pin him there, swaying to
the dance of the sea, in the light of day that reveals those slain
by the sea in the darkness, they take them down one by one
from their gallows and return them to the sea, which has taken
them, sea on all sides, there is no land, there is no ship on the
horizon, nothing—and it is against that landscape of corpses
and nothingness that a man makes a way for himself among
the others and without a word lets himself slip into the water
and begins to swim, he simply *goes away*, and others see him and
follow, and in truth some do not even swim, they just let themselves drop into the sea, without moving, they vanish—it is
even *sweet* to see them—they embrace before giving themselves

to the sea—tears on the faces of men unlooked for—then they let themselves drop into the sea and draw the salt water deep into their lungs so as to sear everything, everything—no one stops them, no one

First is my name, second those eyes, third a thought, fourth the night to come, fifth those mangled bodies, and sixth is *hunger*—hunger that grows inside and gnaws at the throat and settles upon the eyes, five casks of wine and a single sack of ship's biscuits, says Corréard, the cartographer: We cannot go on—the men are watching one another, studying one another, it is the moment that will decide *how* the fight will be, if there is to be a fight, says Lheureux, the first officer: One ration for every man, two glasses of wine and a biscuit—they are watching one another, the men, perhaps it is the light or the sea's idle swaying, like a truce, or the words that Lheureux is pronouncing, standing on a cask: We shall save ourselves, out of the hatred we bear those who have abandoned us, and we shall return to look them in the eye, and nevermore shall they be able to sleep or live or escape the curse that we shall be for them, us, alive, and them, slain every day, forever, by their guilt—perhaps it is that silent light or the sea's idle swaying, like a truce, but what happens is that the men fall silent and desperation becomes docility and order and calm—they file by in front of us one by one, their hands, our hands, a ration for one—almost an absurdity, it comes to mind, in the heart of the sea, over a hundred men defeated, lost, defeated, they form an orderly line, a perfect pattern in the directionless chaos of the womb of the sea, to survive, silently, with inhuman patience, and inhuman reason

First is my name, second those eyes, third a thought, fourth the night to come, fifth those mangled bodies, sixth is hunger and seventh is horror, *the horror,* that breaks out at night——the night again——the horror, the ferocity, the blood, the dying, the hatred, fetid horror. They took possession of a cask, and the wine took possession of them. Under the light of the moon a man is hacking mightily at the lashings of the raft with an ax, an officer tries to stop him, they jump on him and stab him, he turns back toward us, bleeding, we pull out our sabers and muskets, the moonlight disappears behind a cloud, it's hard to understand, it's an endless instant, then an invisible wave of bodies and screams and weapons beating down on us, the blind desperation that seeks death, instantly and be done with it, and the hatred that seeks an enemy, instantly, to drag down to hell——and in the light's coming and going I remember those bodies running onto our sabers and the crackle of musket fire, and the blood spurting from the wounds, and feet slipping on heads crushed between the boards of the raft, and desperate men dragging themselves along on broken legs until they reach one of us and, unarmed by then, sinking their teeth into our legs and hanging on, waiting for the blow and the blade that cleaves them, and in the end——I remember——two of ours dying, literally bitten to death by that inhuman beast come out of the void of the night, and dozens of them dying, lacerated and drowned, dragging themselves around the raft, staring hypnotized at their mutilations, they call on the saints while they plunge their hands into the wounds of our men to rip out their guts—I remember—a man hurling himself on me, squeezing my neck between his hands, and while he is trying to strangle me he never stops whining "mercy, mercy, mercy," absurd spectacle, my life is beneath his fingers, and his rests on the point of my saber that finally cuts into his side and then his belly and then his throat and then his head that rolls into the water and then into what remains, a bloody mess, crumpled between the boards of the raft, a useless puppet into which I steep my saber once, and twice and three and four and five times

First is my name, second those eyes, third a thought, fourth the night to come, fifth those mangled bodies, sixth is hunger, seventh horror, and eighth the ghosts of madness, they flower on that species of slaughter, horrid battlefield rinsed by the waves, bodies everywhere, bits of bodies, greenish, yellowish faces, blood clotted on eyes without pupils, open mouths like wounds and wounds like open mouths, like corpses vomited up by the earth, a disjointed earthquake of the dead, the dying, paved with torments trapped in the precarious skeleton of the raft on which the living—*the living*— prowl, robbing the dead of worthless trifles but above all evaporating into madness one by one, each man in his own way, each with his own phantasms, extorted from the mind by hunger, and by thirst, and by fear, and by desperation. Phantasms. All those who see land—land!—or ships on the horizon. They yell, and no one listens to them. One is writing a formal letter of protest to the Admiralty to express his indig-

nation and denounce the infamy and officially request . . .
Words, prayers, visions, a school of flying fish, a cloud point-
ing the way to salvation, mothers, brothers, wives appearing to
dry the wounds and proffer water and caresses, one is franti-
cally searching for his mirror, his mirror, who has seen his mirror, give me back my mirror, a mirror, my mirror, a man is
blessing the dying with curses and groans, and someone is
talking to the sea in a low voice, talking to it, seated on the
edge of the raft, he is courting it, one would say, and listening
to its replies, the sea replying, a dialogue, the last, in the end
some give in to its cunning replies and, finally convinced, they
let themselves slip into the water to give themselves up to the
great friend who devours them and carries them far away—
while on the raft, backward and forward, endlessly runs Léon,
Léon the little boy, Léon the cabin boy, Léon who is twelve
years old, and madness has taken him, terror has stolen him
away, and he is running backward and forward from one side
of the raft to the other, screaming unceasingly in one long
breath mother of mine, mother of mine, mother of mine,
mother of mine, Léon of the gentle gaze and the velvety skin,
runs like mad, a bird in a cage, until it kills him, his heart, or
who knows what, bursts inside, who knows what it was to
make him drop like that, suddenly, with his eyes rolling and a
convulsion in the chest that shakes him and then hurls him
motionless to the ground whence he is picked up by the arms
of Gilbert—Gilbert who loved him—that hug him close—
Gilbert who loved him and now weeps for him and kisses him,
inconsolable, a strange thing to see, there in the middle, in the
middle of hell, the face of that old man bent over the lips of

that young lad, a strange thing to see those kisses, how can I forget them, I who have seen them, those kisses, I who have no phantasms, I who have death upon me and not even the mercy of some ghost or a sweet madness, I who have ceased counting the days, but know that every night, again, that beast will emerge, it must emerge, the beast of horror, the nightly slaughter, this war we are fighting, this death we are spreading around so as not to die, we who

First is my name, second those eyes, third a thought, fourth the night to come, fifth those mangled bodies, sixth is hunger, seventh is horror, eighth the specters of madness, and ninth is abnormal meat, meat, meat drying on the rigging, meat that bleeds, meat, human meat, in my hands, in my mouth, meat of men that I have seen, men that were, meat of living men now dead, killed, broken, crazed, meat of arms and legs that I have seen fighting, meat stripped from the bone, meat that had a name, and that I now devour maddened with hunger, days spent chewing the leather of our belts and pieces of cloth, on this atrocious raft there is nothing left, nothing, seawater and piss chilled in tin beakers, pieces of tin held under the tongue so as not to go mad with thirst, and shit that you cannot get down, and ropes steeped in blood and salt, the only food that smacks of life, until someone, blinded by hunger, bends over the corpse of a friend and weeping and talking and praying tears the meat from his bones, and like a beast drags it off to a corner and begins to suck it and then bite into it and spew it up and then bite into it again, furiously overcoming the loathing to wrest from death one last shortcut to life, an atrocious road, which however one by one we all take, all of us, equals now inasmuch as we are become beasts and jackals, finally each one silent with his scrap of meat, the bitter taste in the mouth, the hands smeared with blood, in the belly the bite of a blinding pain, the smell of death, the stink, the skin, the meat coming apart, the meat shredding, dripping water and serum, those open bodies, like screams, tables set for the animals we are, the end of everything, horrible surrender, obscene defeat, abominable rout, blasphemous catastrophe, and it is then that I—I—look up—I look up—up—it is then that I look up and I see—I— see it: *the sea.* For the first time, after days and days, I really see it. And I hear its immense voice and powerful smell and, inside, its unstoppable dance, an infinite wave. Everything disappears and nothing remains but the sea, before me, upon me. A revelation. The pall of anguish and fear that has gripped my soul fades away, the web of infamy, cruelty, and horror that has ravished my eyes falls apart, the shadow of death that has devoured my mind dissolves, and in the sudden light of an unexpected clarity I finally see, and hear, and understand. The sea. It had seemed a spectator, even silent, even an accomplice. It had seemed a frame, a stage set, a backdrop. Now I look at it and I see: the sea was everything. It was everything, right from the first moment. I see it dancing around me, sumptuous in an icy light, a marvelous, infinite world. The sea was in the hands that killed, in the dead who were dying, the sea was in the hunger and thirst, the sea was in the torment, in the baseness and the madness, the sea was the hatred and the desperation, mercy and sacrifice, the sea is this blood and this meat, the sea is this horror and this splendor. There is no raft, there are no men, there are no words, feelings, gestures, nothing. There are no guilty and no innocent, condemned and saved. There is only the sea. All things have become the sea. We, the abandoned of the earth, have become the womb of the sea, and the womb of the sea is us, and in us it breathes and lives. I watch it dance in its resplendent mantle for the joy of its own invisible eyes and finally I know that this is the defeat of no man, for it is the triumph of the sea only, all this, and thy glory, and so, so let it be HOSANNA, HOSANNA TO THEE, ocean sea, powerful beyond all powers and marvelous beyond all marvels, HOSANNA AND GLORY TO THEE, master and slave, victim and persecutor, HOSANNA, the earth bows at thy passing and brushes the hem of thy mantle with perfumed lips, HOLY, HOLY, HOLY, womb of every new birth and belly of every death, HOSANNA AND GLORY BE THINE, refuge of all destinies and hearts that breathe, beginning and end, horizon and source, master of nothing, master of all, let it be HOSANNA AND GLORY TO THEE, lord of time and master of the nights, the one and the only, HOSANNA, because thine is the horizon, and dizzyingly deep is thy womb, deep and unfathomable, and GLORY, GLORY, GLORY, to the heavens on high for there is no sky that is not reflected and lost in Thee, nor is there land that may not surrender to Thee, the invincible, the beloved spouse of the moon and kind father of the gentle tides, let all men bow down before Thee and lift up their song of HOSANNA AND GLORY since Thou art within them, and groweth in them, and in Thee they live and die, and for them Thou art the secret and the end and the truth and the judgment and the salvation and the only road for eternity, and thus it is, and thus shall it ever be, until the end of days, which shall be the end of the sea, if the sea shall have an end, Thou, the Holy, the One and Only, Ocean Sea, wherefore let it be HOSANNA AND GLORY until the end of centuries. AMEN.

Amen.

Amen.

Amen.

Amen.

Amen.

Amen.

Amen.

Amen.

Amen.

Amen.

First

      first is my name,

                 first is my name, second those eyes,

    first is my name, second those eyes, third a thought, fourth the coming of the night,

                 first is my name, second those eyes, third a thought, fourth the coming of the night, fifth those mangled bodies, sixth is hunger

                 first is my name, second those eyes, third a thought, fourth the coming of the night, fifth those mangled bodies, sixth is hunger, seventh is horror, eighth the specters of madness

                 first is my name, second those

eyes, third a thought, fourth the coming of the night, fifth those mangled bodies, sixth is hunger, seventh is horror, eighth the specters of madness, ninth is meat, and tenth is a man who watches me but does not kill me. He is called Thomas. He was the strongest of all of them. Because he was cunning. We have not succeeded in killing him. Lheureux tried, the first night. Corréard tried. But he has seven lives, that man. Around him they are all dead, his shipmates. On the raft there are fifteen men left. And he is one of them. He stayed for a long time in the corner farthest away from us. Then he began to creep, slowly, and to get closer. Every movement is an impossible effort, and I should know because I have lain here motionless since last night, and here I have decided to die. Every word is an atrocious effort and every movement an impossible labor. But he keeps coming closer. He has a knife in his belt. And it is me he wants. I know it.

Who knows how much time has passed. There is no more day, there is no more night, all is motionless silence. We are a drifting graveyard. I opened my eyes and he was here. I do not know if it was a nightmare or real. Perhaps it is only madness, finally a madness come to take me. But if it is madness, it hurts, and there is nothing sweet about it. I wish he would do something, that man. But he carries on looking at me and that's all. Just one more step forward and he could be upon me. I have no more weapons. He has a knife . . . I have no more strength, nothing. He has in his eyes the calm and the strength of an animal stalking its prey. It's incredible how he can still manage to hate, here, in this foul, drifting prison where by now there is only death. It's incredible how he can manage *to remem-*

ber. If only I could manage to speak, if only there were a little life left in me, I would tell him that I had to do it, that there is no mercy, there is no guilt in this inferno and that neither of us is here, but only *the sea*, the ocean sea. I would tell him not to look at me anymore, and to kill me. Please. But I cannot manage to speak. He does not move from there, he does not take his eyes off mine. And he does not kill me. Will all this ever finish?

There is a horrendous silence, on the raft and all around. No one wails anymore. The dead are dead, the living are waiting, that's all. No prayers, no screams, nothing. The sea dances, but slowly, it seems a whispered farewell. I do not feel hunger anymore, or thirst or pain. Everything is only an immense lassitude. I open my eyes. That man is still there. I close them again. Kill me, Thomas, or let me die in peace. You have your revenge by now. Go away. He turns his gaze toward the sea. I am no longer anything. My soul is no longer my soul, my life is no longer my life, do not steal death from me with those eyes.

The sea dances, but slowly.

No prayers, no groans, nothing.

The sea dances, but slowly.

Will he watch me die?

My name is Thomas. And this is the story of an abomination. I am writing it in my mind, now, with what strength I have left and with my eyes fixed on that man who shall never have my forgiveness. Death shall read it.

The *Alliance* was a big, strong ship. The sea would never have bested her. It takes three thousand oaks to build a ship like that. A floating forest. It was the idiocy of men that was her undoing. Captain Chaumareys consulted the charts and sounded the depth of the sea floor. But he could not read the sea. He could not read its colors. The *Alliance* wound up on the Arguin sandbank and no one could do anything to stop it. A strange shipwreck: we heard what seemed a dull groan rise up from the bowels of the hull and then the ship stopped dead, listing slightly to one side. Motionless. Forever. I have seen splendid ships struggle against ferocious storms, and I have seen some others surrender and disappear beneath waves tall as castles. It was like a duel. Very beautiful. But the *Alliance* was unable to fight. A silent end. The great sea all around her was almost flat calm. The enemy was within her, not before her. And all her strength was as nothing, against an enemy like that. I have seen many lives wrecked in that absurd way. But ships, never.

The hull was beginning to creak. They decided to abandon the *Alliance* to her fate and they built that raft. It smacked of death before it was even lowered into the water. The men sensed it and thronged around the longboats, to flee from that trap. They had to point the muskets at them to force them to board it. The captain promised and swore that he would not abandon them, that the longboats would tow the raft, that there was no danger. They ended up, packed together like animals, aboard that barge without sides, without a keel, without a helm. And I was one of them. There were soldiers and sailors. A few passengers. And then four officers, a cartographer, and a doctor called Savigny: they occupied the middle of the raft, where the supplies had been put, those few supplies that had not been lost in the confusion of the transshipment. They were standing on a large chest; we were all around them, with the water up to our knees because the raft was wallowing under our weight. I should have understood everything right from that moment.

Of those moments, an image remains. Schmalz. Schmalz the governor, the one who was to take possession of the new colonies in the king's name. They lowered him from the starboard side, seated in his armchair. The armchair, in velvet and gold, and him seated upon it, impassive. They lowered them down as if they were one single statue. We, on that raft, still moored to the *Alliance*, but already at grips with the sea and fear. And him there, descending, hanging in space, toward his longboat, seraphic, like those angels that come down from the ceilings of the theaters in the city. He was swinging, he and his armchair, like a pendulum. And I thought: He is swinging like a hanged man in the evening breeze.

I don't know the precise moment when they abandoned us. I was struggling to keep my feet and to keep Thérèse close to me. But I heard cries, and then shots. I looked up. And above dozens of bobbing heads, and dozens of hands that sawed the air, I saw the sea, and longboats far off, and nothing between us and them. I looked on, incredulous. I knew that they would not return. We were in the hands of destiny. Only luck could save us. But the defeated never have any luck.

Thérèse was but a lass. I don't know how old she was, really. But she seemed a lass. When I was at Rochefort working in the port, she would pass by with her baskets of fish and she would look at me. She looked at me until I fell in love with her. She was all I had, down there. My life, for what it was worth, and her. When I enlisted in the expedition to the new colonies, I managed to have her hired as a sutler. And so we left, both of us on board the *Alliance*. It seemed like a game. When I come to think of it, in those first days, it seemed a game. If I know what it means to be happy, in those nights, we were happy. When I ended up among those who had to board the raft, Thérèse wanted to come with me. She could have boarded a longboat, but she wanted to come with me. I told her that it was madness, that we would meet again on shore, that she had nothing to fear. But she would not listen to me. There were big men hard as rock whimpering and begging for a place on those cursed longboats, jumping down from the raft and risking getting themselves killed just to escape from there. But she, she boarded the raft without a word, hiding all her fears. They do things, women, at times, that are enough to leave you high and dry. You could spend a lifetime trying, but you would never have that buoyancy they have, at times. They are buoyant inside. Buoyant.

The first ones died at night, dragged into the sea by the waves that swept the raft. In the darkness, you could hear their cries gradually fading away. At dawn, about ten men were missing. Some lay trapped between the boards of the raft, trampled by the others. The four officers, together with Corréard, the cartographer, and Savigny, the doctor, took the situation in hand. They had the weapons. And they controlled the supplies. The men trusted them. Lheureux, one of the officers, even made a fine speech, he had a sail hoisted and said, "It will carry us to land and there we shall follow those who have betrayed and abandoned us and we shall not rest until they have tasted our revenge." That's precisely what he said: until they have tasted our revenge. He didn't even seem like an officer. He seemed like one of us. The men were heartened by those words. We all thought that it would really end like that. All we had to do was stand fast and not be afraid. The sea had subsided. A light wind filled our makeshift sail. Each of us had his ration of food and drink. Thérèse said to me, "We'll make it." And I said, "Yes."

It was at sunset that the officers, without a word, pushed one of the three wine casks down from the big chest, so that it rolled into our midst. They didn't lift a finger when some threw themselves upon it, opened it, and began drinking. The men were running toward the cask, there was a great turmoil, everyone wanted that wine, and I didn't understand. I remained motionless, holding Thérèse close to me. There was something strange about all that. Then you could hear shouting and the blows of an ax with which someone was trying to cleave the lashings that held the raft together. It was like a signal. A savage fight broke out. It was dark; only occasionally did the moon emerge from behind the clouds. I could hear the crackle of musketry, and, like apparitions, in those sudden blades of light, men hurled themselves upon one another and on the corpses, and sabers struck out blindly. Screams, furious shouts, and groans. All I had was a knife: the same one that now I will plunge into the heart of this man who no longer has the strength to escape. I gripped it, but I didn't know who the enemy was, I didn't want to kill, I didn't understand. Then the moon came out once more, and I saw: an unarmed man who was hanging on to Savigny, the doctor, and shouting mercy, mercy, mercy, and he didn't stop screaming when the first saber stroke cut into his belly, and then the second and the third . . . I saw him slump to the deck. I saw Savigny's face. And I understood. Who the enemy was. And that the enemy would win.

When the light returned, in an atrocious dawn, there were dozens of corpses on the raft, horribly mutilated, and dying men everywhere. Around the big chest, about thirty armed men guarded the supplies. In the officers' eyes there was a kind of euphoric confidence. They strolled around the raft, with sabers unsheathed, calming the living and throwing the dying into the water. No one dared say anything. The terror and bewilderment created by that night of hatred silenced and paralyzed everyone. No one yet really understood what had happened. I watched all that, and I thought: If this carries on, we have no hope. The most senior officer was called Dupont. He passed close by me, with his white uniform soiled with blood, blathering something about the duties of a soldier and I don't know what else. He had a pistol in his hand and his saber in its scabbard. He turned his back on me for a moment. I knew that he wouldn't give me another chance. He found himself immobilized with a knife at his throat before he even had time to shout. From the big chest, the men instinctively pointed their muskets at us. They would have shot, too, but Savigny yelled at them to hold their fire. And then, in the silence, it was my turn to speak, with the point of my knife pressed against Dupont's throat. And I said, "They are killing us, one by one. And they will not stop until they are the only ones left. Last night they got you drunk . . . but the next time they will have no need of excuses or help. They have the weapons and we are many no longer. In the dark, they will do what they want. You may believe me or not, but that's the way it is. There aren't enough supplies for everybody, and they know it. They will not leave a single man alive that they don't need. You may believe me or not, but that's the way it is."

The men around me were as if stunned. Hunger, thirst, the battle in the night, that sea that never ceased its dancing . . . They tried to think, they wanted to understand. Lost, there, struggling against death, it was hard to accept the presence of another, even more insidious enemy: men like you. Against you. There was something absurd about all that. And yet it was true. One by one, they closed ranks around me. Savigny was shouting threats and orders. But no one was listening to him. Idiotic as it may have seemed, a war was breaking out on that raft, lost at sea. We returned the officer, Dupont, alive in exchange for some victuals and arms. We huddled in a corner of the raft. And we waited for the night. I kept Thérèse close to me. She kept on saying, "I'm not afraid. I'm not afraid."

I don't want to remember that night, and the others that followed. A meticulous, expert massacre. The more time passed, the more it became necessary for our survival that our numbers be limited to a few. And they, scientifically, were killing. There was something about that calculated clarity, that pitiless intelligence, that fascinated me. Amid all that desperation, an extraordinary mind was required if the logical thread of that extermination was not to be lost. In the eyes of this man, which watch me now as if I were a dream, I have read, a thousand times, with hatred and admiration, the signs of a horrendous brilliance.

We tried to defend ourselves. But it was impossible. The weak can only run away. And you cannot run away from a raft lost in the middle of the sea. By day we struggled against hunger, desperation, madness. Then night fell and the war flared up again, a war that grew more and more tired, exhausted, made of slower and slower gestures, fought by dying murderers, and beasts in their death throes. At daybreak, new deaths sustained the hopes of the living and their horrendous plans for salvation. I don't know how long all this lasted. But it had to end, sooner or later, in one way or another. And it ended. The water was finished, the wine, and what little was left to eat. No ship had arrived to save us. There was no time left for any calculations. There was nothing left to kill one another for. I saw two officers throw their weapons into the water and wash themselves for hours, maniacally, with seawater. They wanted to die innocent. That was what remained of their ambition and their intelligence. All useless. That massacre, their infamous conduct, our fury. All perfectly useless. No intelligence and no courage may change fate. I remember that I sought Savigny's face. And I saw, finally, the face of a defeated man. Now I know that even when hovering on the verge of death, men's faces are still lies.

That night I opened my eyes, awakened by a sound, and in the uncertain light of the moon I glimpsed the silhouette of a man, standing in front of me. Instinctively I grasped my knife and pointed it at him. The man stopped. I didn't know if it was a dream, a nightmare, or what. Somehow I had to manage to keep my eyes open. I stayed there motionless. Seconds, minutes, I don't know. Then the man turned. And I saw two things. A face, and it was that of Savigny, and a saber that slashed the air as it plunged down toward me. It was a moment. I didn't know if it was a dream, a nightmare, or what. I felt no pain, nothing. There was no blood on me. The man disappeared. I stayed there motionless. Only after a little did I turn and see: there was Thérèse, stretched out alongside me, with a wound that had slashed open her breast and her eyes staring, staring at me, stupefied. No. It couldn't be true. No. Now it was all over. Why? It must be a dream, a nightmare, he couldn't have done it really. No. Not now, no. Why now?

"Farewell, my love."

"Oh no, no, no, no."

"Farewell."

"You shall not die, I swear."

"Farewell."

"I beg you, you shall not die . . ."

"Leave me."

"You shall not die."

"Leave me."

"We shall be saved, you must believe me."

"My love . . ."

"Do not die . . ."

"My love."

"Do not die. Do not die. Do not die."

The sound of the sea was very loud. Louder than I had ever heard it. I took her in my arms and dragged myself right to the edge of the raft. I let her slip into the water. I did not want her to stay in that hell. And if there was not a speck of earth there to watch over her rest, then let the deep sea take her to itself. Boundless garden of the dead, without crosses or confines. She slipped away like a wave, only more beautiful than the others.

I don't know. It's hard to understand all this. If I had a life ahead of me, perhaps I would spend it telling this story, without ever stopping, a thousand times until one day I would understand it. But ahead of me there is only a man who awaits my knife.

And then sea, sea, sea.

The only person who ever really taught me anything, an old man called Darrell, always used to say that there were three types of men: those who live in front of the sea, those who venture into the sea, and those who manage to return from the sea, alive. And he used to say, "What a surprise you'll get when you find out who are the happiest." I was a young lad then. In winter I would look at the ships hauled up on the beach, supported by enormous wooden props, their hulls exposed and their keels cutting the sand like useless blades. And I would think: I'm not going to stop here. I want to venture into the sea. Because if there's something true in this world, it's down there. Now I'm down there, in the deepest part of the womb of the sea. I am still alive because I have killed without mercy, because I eat this meat ripped from the corpses of my shipmates, because I have drunk their blood. I have seen an infinity of things that are invisible from the shores of the sea. I have seen what desire really is, and fear. I have seen men fall apart and turn into children. And then change again and become ferocious beasts. I have seen marvelous dreams dreamed, and I have listened to the most beautiful stories of my life, told by ordinary men, a moment before they threw themselves into the sea to vanish forever. I have read signs I didn't know in the sky and stared at the horizon with eyes I didn't think I had. I have understood the true nature of hatred on these bloodstained boards, where the seawater makes wounds putrefy. And as for compassion, I didn't know what it was until I saw our murderers' hands spend hours stroking the hair of a mate who could not manage to die. I have seen ferocity, as men kicked the dying off the raft; I have seen sweetness, in Gilbert's eyes as he kissed his little Léon; I have seen intelligence, in the gestures with which Savigny embroidered his massacre; and I have seen madness, in those two men who spread their wings one morning and flew away, into the sky. Were I to live for another thousand years, love would be the name of the light weight that was Thérèse, in my arms, before she slipped into the waves. And destiny would be the name of this ocean sea, infinite and beautiful. I wasn't wrong, back ashore, during those winters, when I thought that truth lay here. It took me years to descend to the farthest depths of the womb of the sea: but what I was looking for, I found. True things. Even the most intolerable, atrocious truth of all. This sea is a mirror. Here, in its womb, I have seen myself. I have really seen.

I don't know. If I had a life ahead of me—I who am about to die—I would spend it telling this story, without ever stopping, a thousand times, so as to understand why truth gives itself over only to horror, and to arrive at it we have had to pass through this inferno, to see it we have had to destroy one another, to have it we have had to become ferocious beasts, to flush it out we have had to rack ourselves with pain. And to be true men we have had to die. Why? Why do things become true only in the grip of desperation? Who has turned the world around this way, so that the truth must be on the dark side, and the repulsive swamp of forsaken humanity is the only loathsome earth in which there grows the only thing that is not a lie? And in the end: What truth can this be, that stinks of corpses, and flourishes in blood, feeds on pain, and lives where man humiliates himself, and triumphs where man rots? *Whose* truth is this? Is it a truth *for us*? Back ashore, during those winters, I use to imagine a truth that was tranquillity, womb, alleviation, mercy, and sweetness. It was a truth made for us. Which expected us, and would have looked down on us, like a mother found anew. But here, in the womb of the sea, I have seen truth make its nest, meticulous and perfect: and what I saw was a bird of prey, magnificent in flight, and ferocious. I don't know. This wasn't what I dreamed of, in the winter, when I used to dream of this.

Darrell was one of those who returned. He had seen the womb of the sea, he had been here, but he had returned. People said he was a man beloved of the gods. He had survived two shipwrecks and, they said, the second time he had done over three thousand miles, in a piddling little boat, before he found land again. Days and days in the womb of the sea. And then he returned. That's why people would say, "Darrell is wise, Darrell has seen, Darrell knows." I would spend days listening to his talk, but he never told me anything about the womb of the sea. He didn't like to talk about it. He didn't even

like the fact that people would hold him to be wise and sagacious. Above all, he couldn't stand that someone could say of
him that *he had saved himself.* He could not bear to *hear* that word:
saved. He would lower his head and half shut his eyes, in a way
that was impossible to forget. I would look at him, in those
moments, and I couldn't manage to put a name to what I read
on his face, and that—I knew—was his secret. A thousand
times that name was on the tip of my tongue. Here, on this
raft, in the womb of the sea, it has come to me. And now I
know that Darrell was a wise and sagacious man. A man who
had seen. But, before all other things, and to the depths of his
every instant, he was an *inconsolable* man. This is what the womb
of the sea has taught me. Those who have seen the truth will
always be *inconsolable.* Only he who has never been in danger is
really *saved.* A ship might even appear, now, on the horizon, and
speed here on the waves to arrive a second before death and
take us away, and have us return alive, alive—but this would
not save us, really. Even if we ever found ourselves ashore
somewhere again, we shall never again be saved. And what we
have seen will remain in our eyes, what we have done will
remain on our hands, what we have felt will remain in our
souls. And forever, we who have known the truth, forever, we
the children of horror, forever, we the veterans of the womb of
the sea, forever, we the wise and the sagacious, forever—we
shall be inconsolable.

Inconsolable.

Inconsolable.

There is a great silence aboard the raft. Every so often Savigny opens his eyes and looks at me. We are so close to death,

we are so deep in the womb of the sea, that not even faces manage to lie anymore. His was so true. Fear, fatigue, and disgust. Who knows what he reads on mine? He is so close, now, that sometimes I can smell him. Now I shall drag myself over there, and with my knife I shall split his heart. What a strange duel. For days, on a raft at the mercy of the sea, among all possible forms of death, we have continued to seek each other out and to strike at each other. Weaker and weaker, slower and slower. And now, this last stab seems eternal. But it will not be. I swear it. May no fate harbor any illusions: omnipotent though it may be, it will not arrive in time to stop this duel. He will not die before he is killed. And before I die, I shall kill him. It is all I have left: Thérèse's light weight, printed like an indelible wave in my arms, and the need, the lust, for any kind of justice. Let this sea know that I shall have it. Let any sea know that I will get there before it. And it will not be among its waves that Savigny shall pay, but at my hands.

There is a great silence aboard the raft. Only the sound of the sea can be heard. Very loud.

FIRST IS MY NAME, second those eyes, third a thought, fourth the coming of the night, fifth those mangled bodies, sixth is hunger, seventh is horror, eighth the specters of madness, ninth is meat, and tenth is a man who watches me but does not kill me.

The last is a sail.

White. On the horizon.

BOOK III

The Songs of the Return

CHAPTER I

Elisewin

PERCHED ON THE EDGE of the land, a stone's throw from the stormy sea, the Almayer Inn lay motionless, immersed in the dark of the night like a portrait, a love token, in the darkness of a drawer.

Although dinner had been over for some time, everyone, inexplicably, was lingering in the large room with the fireplace. The sea's fury, outside, troubled the spirit and set ideas in disarray.

"It's not for me to say, but perhaps we ought to . . ."

"Have no fear, Bartleboom. In general, inns do not get shipwrecked."

"In general? What do you mean, *in general*?"

But strangest of all were the children. They were all there, with their noses pressed up against the windows, oddly silent, watching the darkness outside: Dood, who lived on Bartleboom's windowsill, and Ditz, who granted Father Pluche his dreams, and Dol, who saw the ships for Plasson. And Dira. There was even the beautiful little girl who slept in Ann Deverià's bed and who no one had ever seen walking around the inn. All there, hypnotized by who knows what, silent and restless.

"They are like little animals, believe me. They sense the danger. It's instinct."

"Plasson, why don't you do something to calm your friend?"

"I say, that little girl is splendid . . ."

"You try, Madame."

"There is absolutely no need for anyone to take trouble to calm me, since I am perfectly calm."

"Calm?"

"Perfectly."

"Elisewin . . . isn't she beautiful? She seems . . ."

"Father Pluche, you must stop looking at women all the time."

"She is not a woman . . ."

"Oh yes, she is."

"A small one, though . . ."

"Let's say that the dictates of common sense warrant due prudence in considering . . ."

"That's not common sense. That's plain fear."

"That's not true."

"Yes."

"No."

"It certainly is."

"It certainly isn't."

"Oh, enough. You two are capable of going on for hours. I shall retire."

"Good night, Madame," said everybody.

"Good night," replied Ann Deverià, a trifle absently. But she did not get out of her armchair. She did not even change position. She stayed there, motionless. As if nothing had happened. Really, it was a strange night, that one.

Perhaps, in the end, they would all have surrendered to the normality of a night like any other; one by one, they would have gone up to their rooms, they would even have fallen asleep, despite that tireless roaring of the stormy sea, each one wrapped up in his dreams, or hidden in a wordless sleep. Perhaps, in the end, it could have even become a night like any other. But it didn't.

The first to take her eyes off the windows, to turn suddenly and to run out of the room, was Dira. The other children followed her, without a word. Speechless, Plasson looked at Bartleboom, who, speechless, looked at Father Pluche, who, speechless, looked at Elisewin, who, speechless, looked at Ann Deverià, who carried on looking straight ahead. But with an imperceptible surprise. When the children reentered the room they were carrying lanterns in their hands. Dira set to lighting them, one by one, in a strange frenzy.

"Has something happened?" asked Bartleboom politely.

"Hold this," replied Dood, proffering him a lighted lantern. "And you, Plasson, hold this, quick."

No one knew what was going on anymore. Everyone found himself holding a lighted lantern. No one explained anything; the children were running here and there as if devoured by an incomprehensible anxiety. Father Pluche was staring at the little flame of his lantern as if hypnotized. Bartleboom was mumbling vague phonemes of protest. Ann Deverià got out of her armchair. Elisewin realized she was trembling. It was in that moment that the big glass door that gave onto the beach was thrown wide open. As if catapulted into the room, a raging wind began running around everything and everybody. The children's faces lit up. And Dira said, "Quick . . . this way!"

She ran out of the open door, with her lantern in hand.

"Let's go . . . out, out of here!"

The children were shouting. But not with fear. They were shouting to be heard above the roaring of sea and wind. But it was a kind of joy—an inexplicable joy—that rang out in their voices.

Bartleboom remained standing, rigid, in the middle of the room, completely disoriented. Father Pluche turned toward Elisewin: he saw that her face was alarmingly pale. Madame Deverià did not say a word, but took her lantern and followed Dira. Plasson ran after her.

"Elisewin, it would be better if you stayed here . . ."

"No."

"Elisewin, now listen to me . . ."

Mechanically, Bartleboom took his cloak and ran out mumbling to himself.

"Elisewin . . ."

"Let's go."

"No, listen to me . . . I am not at all sure that you . . ."

The little girl—the very beautiful one—came back and, without saying a word, took Elisewin by the hand, smiling at her.

"But I am sure, Father Pluche."

Her voice was trembling. But it was trembling with strength and will. Not with fear.

The Almayer Inn stayed behind, with its door banging in the wind, and its lights dwindling in the dark. Like sparks shooting out of a brazier, ten little lanterns went running along the beach, drawing witty and secret hieroglyphics in the night. The sea, invisible, was churning out an unbelievable din. The wind was blowing, throwing worlds, faces, and thoughts into disorder. Marvelous wind. And ocean sea.

"I demand to know where the devil we are going!"

"Eh?"

"WHERE THE DEVIL ARE WE GOING?"

"Keep that lantern up, Bartleboom!"

"The lantern!"

"Hey, do we really have to run like this?"

"I haven't run for years . . ."

"Years what?"

"Good heavens, Dood, might one know . . ."

"HAVEN'T RUN FOR YEARS."

"Everything all right, Bartleboom?"

"Dood, good heavens . . ."

"Elisewin!"

"I'm here, I'm here."

"Let's stay close, Elisewin."

"I'm here."

Marvelous wind. Ocean sea.

"Do you know what I think?"

"What?"

"According to me, it's for the ships. THE SHIPS."

"The ships?"

"That's what you do when there is a storm . . . You light fires along the coast for the ships . . . so that they don't end up on the coast . . ."

"Bartleboom, did you hear?"

"Eh?"

"You are about to become a hero, Bartleboom!"

"What the devil is Plasson saying?"

"That you are about to become a hero!"

"Me?"

"MISS DIRA!"

"Where's he off to?"

"Couldn't we stop for a bit?"

"Do you know what the inhabitants of the island do, when there is a storm?"

"No, Madame."

"They run like mad up and down the island with lanterns held above their heads . . . and so the ships . . . and so the ships don't know what's going on and they wind up on the rocks."

"You're joking."

"I'm not joking in the slightest . . . There are whole islands that live off what they find in the wrecks."

"You don't mean to say that . . ."

"Hold the lantern for me, please."

"Will you stop a minute, good Lord!"

"Madame . . . your cloak!"

"Leave it there."

"But . . ."

"Leave it there, for heaven's sake!"

Marvelous wind. Ocean sea.

"But what are they doing?"

"Miss Dira!"

"Where the devil are they going?"

"For goodness' sake . . ."

"DOOD!"

"Run, Bartleboom."

"Yes, but which way?"

"Oh, for goodness' sake, have these children lost their tongues?"

"Look there."

"It's Dira."

"She's going up the hill."

"I'm going that way."

"Dood! Dood! We ought to go toward the hill!"

"Where's he going?"

"Christ, does anybody know what's going on around here?"

"Keep that lantern up and run, Father Pluche."

"I shall not take one more step until . . ."

"But why won't they speak?"

"I don't like that look of theirs one little bit."

"What don't you like?"

"The eyes. THE EYES!"

"Plasson, where has Plasson got to?"

"I'm going with Dol."

"But . . ."

"MY LANTERN, MY LANTERN HAS GONE OUT!"

"Madame Deverià, where are you going?"

"At least tell me if I'm about to save a ship or wreck one!"

"ELISEWIN! My lantern! It's gone out!"

"Plasson, what did Dira say?"

"That way, that way . . ."

"My lantern . . ."

"MADAME!"

"She cannot hear you anymore, Bartleboom."

"But it's not possible . . ."

"ELISEWIN! Where has Elisewin got to? My lantern . . ."

"Father Pluche, come away from there."

"My lantern has gone out."

"To blazes with it, I'm going that way."

"Come, I'll light it for you."

"My God, Elisewin, have you seen her?"

"She must have gone with Madame Deverià."

"But she was here, she was here . . ."

"Hold that lantern upright."

"Elisewin . . ."

"Ditz, have you seen Elisewin?"

"DITZ! DITZ! What the devil has got into these children?"

"Here . . . your lantern . . ."

"I don't understand what's going on."

"Come on, let's go."

"I must find Elisewin . . ."

"Let's go, Father Pluche, everyone else is already ahead."

"Elisewin . . . ELISEWIN! Good God, where have you got to? . . . ELISEWIN!"

"Enough, Father Pluche, we'll find her . . ."

"ELISEWIN! ELISEWIN! Elisewin, I beg you . . ."

Motionless, holding her spent lantern, Elisewin heard her name come from afar, commingled with the wind and the roar of the sea. In the darkness, ahead of her, she could see the tiny lights of many lanterns as they met, each one lost in its own journey around the edge of the storm. In her mind there was neither anxiety nor fear. A placid lake had suddenly exploded in her soul. It had the same sound of a voice she recognized.

She turned and slowly retraced her steps. The wind was no more, the night was no more, the sea was no more, for her. She was going, and she knew where. That was all. A marvelous feeling. As when destiny finally shows its hand, and becomes a clear path, and an unequivocal trail, and a certain direction. The interminable moment of drawing near. That coming close. One would like it never to stop. The gesture of giving oneself over to destiny. Now that is an emotion. With no more dilemmas, no more untruths. Knowing where it lies. And attaining it. Whatever it may be, destiny.

She was walking—and it was the most beautiful thing she had ever done.

She saw the Almayer Inn drawing nearer. Its lights. She left the beach, crossed the threshold, entered and closed the door behind her, that same door from which she had rushed out together with the others, who knows how long before, still all unknowing.

Silence.

On the wooden floor, one step after another. Grains of sand crunching underfoot. On the floor, in a corner, Plasson's cloak, which he had dropped in his haste to run off. On the cushions of the armchair, the impression of Madame Deverià's body, as if she had just got up. And in the center of the room, motionless, Adams. Who was looking at her.

One step after another, until she was close to him. And said to him, "You won't hurt me, will you?"

You won't hurt her, will you?

"No."

No.

Then

Elisewin

took

that man's face

between her hands

and

she kissed it.

In Carewall, they would never stop telling this story. If only they knew it. They would never stop. Each in his own way, but they would all carry on telling the tale of those two and a whole night spent restoring life to each other, with lips and with hands, a young girl who has seen nothing and a man who has seen too much, one inside the other—every inch of skin a journey, of discovery, of homecoming—in Adams's mouth to savor the taste of the world, on Elisewin's breast to forget it—in the womb of that deeply troubled night, black storm, flashes of spume in the darkness, waves like collapsing woodpiles, noise, resounding blasts, raging with sound and speed, hurled onto the veined surface of the sea, the sinews of the world, ocean sea, a drenched colossus, writhing—sighs, sighs in Elisewin's throat—soaring velvet—sighs at each new step in that world that crosses mountains never seen and lakes with forms unimaginable—on Adams's belly the white weight of that young girl swaying to a soundless music—whoever would have said that by kissing the eyes of a man you could see so far away—by caressing the legs of a young girl you could run so fast and escape—escape from everything—to see so far away—they came from the two farthest extremities of life, this is the amazing thing, one would have thought they would never have met, if not by crossing the universe from one end to the other, and instead they did not even have to look for each other, this is the incredible thing, and the only hard thing was recognizing each other, recognizing each other, the work of a moment, at the first glance they already knew, this is the marvelous thing—this is the tale they would continue to tell, forever, in Carewall, so that no one might forget that we are never far enough away to find one another, never—but those two were far enough away—to find each other, far away, farther than any other and now—Elisewin's voice cried out, because of the torrents of stories that are storming her soul, and Adams weeps, as he feels them slipping away, those stories, finished, finally, finished—perhaps the world is a wound

and someone is stitching it up in the fusion of those two bodies—and it is not even love, this is the amazing thing, but it is
hands, and skin, lips, astonishment, sex, tastes—sadness, perhaps—even sadness—desire—when they tell the story they
will not say the word love—they will say a thousand words,
but they will not mention love—all is silent around them,
when suddenly Elisewin feels her back breaking and her mind
fading into white, she holds that man close inside her, clasps
his hands, and thinks: I'll die. She feels her back breaking and
her mind fading into white, she holds that man close inside
her, clasps his hand and, you see, she will not die.

"LISTEN TO ME, Elisewin . . ."
    "No, don't talk."
    "Listen to me."
    "No."
    "What will happen here will be horrible and . . ."
    "Kiss me . . . it's dawn, they'll come back . . ."
    "Listen to me . . ."
    "Don't talk, I beg you."
    "Elisewin . . ."
    What can you do? How can you say what you have to say
to such a woman, with her hands on your body and her skin,
her skin, you cannot talk of death to one like her, how do you
tell such a girl things she already knows and yet it is necessary
for her to listen, to the words, one after another, and that even
if you know yet you must listen, sooner or later, someone must
say them and you must listen to them, she must listen to them,

that young girl who is saying, "I have never seen that look in your eyes before."

And then, "If only you wanted to, you could save yourself."

How do you tell such a woman that you would like to save yourself and, even more, you would like to save her along with you, and do nothing else but save her, and save yourself, for a whole lifetime, but it's not possible, everyone has his own journey to make, and in the arms of a woman you end up following a twisted road, which even you don't understand that well, and when the right time comes, you haven't the words to tell her about it, words that sit well, there, between those kisses and on the skin, there's no way around it, and it's some job searching for them in what you are and what you have felt, you can't find them, they always have the wrong sound, they have no music, there, between those kisses and on the skin, it's a question of music. And so you say something, but it's wretched.

"Elisewin, I shall never be *saved* anymore."

How do you tell such a man that now it is my turn to teach him something and between his caresses I want to make him understand that destiny is not chains but wings, and if only he still had any real will to live he could, and if only he really wanted me he could have another thousand nights like this instead of that one horrible night that he is heading for, only because it is waiting for him, that horrendous night, and has been calling him for years. How do you tell such a man that becoming a murderer will not help and that blood and pain will not help, it's only a way of running at breakneck speed toward the end, when a time and a way to ensure that nothing finishes are here waiting for us, and calling us, if only we could listen to them, if only he could, really, really, *listen to me*. How do you tell such a man that he is losing you?

"I shall go away . . ."

". . ."

"I don't want to be here . . . I'm going away."

". . ."

"I don't want to hear that scream, I want to be far away."

". . ."

"I don't want to hear it."

The truth is that it's the music that's hard, it's the music that's hard to find, to say things, there so close to each other, the music and the gestures, to dissolve the suffering, when there is absolutely nothing to be done anymore, the right music so that it may be a dance, in some way, and not a wrench, that going off, that slipping away, toward life and away from life, strange pendulum of the soul, redeeming and murderous, being able to dance it would hurt less, and that's why lovers, all of them, seek that music, in that moment, within words, in the dust of gestures, and know that, if they had the courage, only silence would be music, precise music, a slow loving silence, glade of farewells and weary lake that finally runs into the span of a tiny melody, learned since the beginning, to be sung in a low voice.

"Farewell, Elisewin."

A tiny little melody.

"Farewell, Thomas."

Elisewin slips out from under the cloak and gets up. Her young girl's body, nude, with only the warmth of an entire night upon her. She picks up her dress and moves over to the windows. The world outside is still there. You can do whatever you like, but you can always be sure that you will find it in its place, always.

It's hard to believe, but that's the way it is.

Two bare feet, young girl's feet. They climb the stairs, enter a room, go toward a window, stop.

The hills are resting. As if there were no sea before them.

"WE SHALL LEAVE tomorrow, Father Pluche."

"What?"

"Tomorrow. We shall leave."

"But . . ."

"Please."

"Elisewin . . . you cannot decide just like that, without warning . . . we have to write to Daschenbach . . . look, they're not sitting there waiting for us every blessed day . . ."

"We are not going to Daschenbach."

"What do you mean, we're not going to Daschenbach?"

"We're not going there."

"Elisewin, let's keep calm. We have come all this way because you must get better, and to get better you must go into the sea, and to go into the sea you must go to . . ."

"I have already gone into the sea."

"Pardon?"

"I no longer have anything to get better from, Father Pluche."

"But . . ."

"I am alive."

"Jesus . . . what the devil has happened?"

"Nothing . . . all you must do is trust me . . . I beg you, you must trust me . . ."

"I . . . I trust you, but . . ."

"Then let me leave. Tomorrow."

"Tomorrow . . ."

Father Pluche stands there, twiddling his astonishment between his fingers. A thousand questions in his head. And he knows very well what he should do. Few words. Clear. A simple thing: "And what will your father say?" A simple thing. And yet it gets lost on the way. There is no way of finding it again. Father Pluche is still there looking for it when he hears his own voice asking, "And how is it? . . . The sea, how is it?"

Elisewin smiles.

"Very beautiful."

"And?"

Elisewin does not stop smiling.

"At a certain point, it ends."

THEY LEFT EARLY in the morning. The carriage bowling along the coast road. Father Pluche let himself be jounced about on his seat with the same cheerful resignation with which he had packed his bags, said good-bye to everybody, said good-bye to everybody again, and deliberately left a suitcase at the inn, because when one leaves, one should always sow an excuse for returning. One never knows. He was silent until he saw the road turn and the sea getting farther away. Not a second longer.

"Would it be too much to ask where we are going?"

Elisewin was holding a sheet of paper firmly in her hand. She glanced at it.

"St. Parteny."

"And what's that?"

"A town," said Elisewin, closing her hand over the paper.

"A town where?"

"It will take about twenty days. It's in the country, near the capital."

"About twenty days? But this is madness."

"Look at the sea, Father Pluche, it's going away."

"About twenty days . . . I trust you have an excellent reason for making a journey of that kind . . ."

"It's going away . . ."

"Elisewin, I'm talking to you, what are we going down there for?"

"We are going to look for somebody."

"A twenty-day journey to *look for* somebody?"

"Yes."

"Good heavens, then he must be a prince at the very least, or for all I know the king in person, a saint . . ."

"More or less . . ."

Pause.

"He's an admiral."

Pause.

"Jesus . . ."

161

IN THE TAMAL ARCHIPELAGO every evening a fog would come up that devoured the ships and restored them at dawn completely covered in snow. In the Cadaoum Strait, at every new moon, the water would retreat leaving behind it an immense sandbank populated by talking molluscs and poisonous seaweed. Off the coast of Sicily an island had disappeared and another two, not shown on the charts, had surfaced not far distant. In the waters of Draghar they had captured the pirate van Dell, who had preferred to throw himself to the sharks rather than fall into the hands of the Royal Navy. In his palace, then, Admiral Langlais was still cataloging with extenuating precision the plausible absurdities and the unlikely truths that reached him from all the seas of the world. His pen traced with immutable patience the fantastic geography of an indefatigable world. His mind was at rest in the precision of an unchanging day-to-day existence. Identical to itself, his life unrolled. And his garden lay untended, almost disturbing.

"My name is Elisewin," said the girl, when she stood before him.

It struck him, that voice: velvet.

"I have known a man named Thomas."

Velvet.

"When he lived here, with you, his name was Adams."

Admiral Langlais remained motionless, holding the look in the girl's dark eyes. He said nothing. He had hoped never to hear that name again. He had kept it far from him for days, months. He had a few moments in which to prevent its returning, to wound his soul and his memories. He thought of getting up and asking that girl to go away. He would give her a carriage. Money. Anything. He would order her to go away. In the king's name, go away.

As if from afar, that velvety voice reached him. And it was saying, "Keep me with you."

For fifty-three days and nine hours, Langlais did not know what had persuaded him in that instant to reply, "Yes, if you wish."

He understood one evening, seated beside Elisewin, listening to that voice recite:

"In Timbuktu, this is the hour in which the women like to sing and make love to their men. They draw the veils aside from their faces and even the sun moves away, dumbfounded at their beauty."

Langlais felt an immense, sweet fatigue steal upon his heart. As if he had wandered for years, lost, and finally found the road back home. He did not turn toward Elisewin. But he said quietly, "How do you know this story?"

"I don't know. But I know that it is yours. This, and all the others."

ELISEWIN STAYED in Langlais's palace for five years. Father Pluche for five days.

On the sixth he said to Elisewin that it was incredible, but he had left a suitcase down there, at the Almayer Inn, incredible, really, but there was some important stuff in there, inside the suitcase, clothes and perhaps even the book with all the prayers.

"What do you mean, *perhaps*?"

"Perhaps . . . that is, certainly, now that I come to think of it, certainly, it's in that suitcase, you understand that I absolutely cannot leave it there . . . not that they're so wonderful, those prayers, for goodness' sake, but, you know, to lose them like that . . . and considering that it's a matter of a little trip of no more than twenty days or so, it's not that far away, it's only a question of . . ."

"Father Pluche . . ."

". . . it's understood that I would come back in any case . . . I'm just going to collect the suitcase, maybe I'll stop to rest for a few days and then . . ."

"Father Pluche . . ."

". . . it's a question of a couple of months at most, perhaps I might pop in on your father, that is, I mean, *ad absurdum*, it would be even better if I . . ."

"Father Pluche . . . God, how I'll miss you."

He left the next day. He was already aboard the carriage when he got out again and, going up to Langlais, said to him, "Do you know something? I would have thought that admirals stayed at sea . . ."

"I would have thought that priests stayed in church."

"Oh well, you know, God is everywhere . . ."

"So is the sea, Father, so is the sea."

He left. And he didn't leave a suitcase behind, this time.

Elisewin stayed in Langlais's palace for five years. The meticulous order of those rooms and the silence of that life reminded her of the white carpets of Carewall, and the circular avenues, and the flowerless life that her father, one day, had prepared for her. But what had been medicine and cure down there, here was a clear certainty and a joyful recovery. What she had known as the womb of a weakness, here she was rediscovering as the form of a crystalline strength. From Langlais she learned that, among all possible lives, you have to anchor yourself to one to be able to contemplate all the others with serenity. One by one, she gave Langlais the thousand stories that one man and one night had sown in her, God knows how, but in an indelible and definitive way. He would listen to her, in silence. She would narrate. Velvet.

They never talked of Adams. Only once did Langlais, suddenly looking up from his books, say slowly, "I *loved* that man, if you can understand what that means, I *loved* him."

Langlais died one summer morning, devoured by abominable pain and accompanied by a voice—velvet—that was telling him of the scents of a garden, the smallest and most beautiful in Timbuktu.

Elisewin left the next day. She wanted to go back to Carewall. It would take her a month, or a lifetime, but there she would return. Of what awaited her there, she could imagine but little. She only knew that she would keep all those stories within her for herself and forever. She knew that in any man she might come to love, she would seek the flavor of Thomas. And she knew that no land could obscure, in her, the *mark* of the sea.

All the rest was still nothing. *To invent it*—that would have been marvelous.

~

CHAPTER 2

Father Pluche

A Prayer for One Who Is Lost, and Therefore, to Tell the Truth, a Prayer for Me.

Have patience, do
O Lord Most High
For once again it is I.

So, things are
going pretty well here,
the fact is that
folk get by,
some better than others,
but one always finds a way

a way to manage,
you understand me,
but this isn't the problem.
The problem is quite different,
if you have the patience to listen
to listen to me,
to.
The problem is this road
this fine road
this road that rolls
and unrolls
and upholds
but does not roll straight
as it could
and not even crooked
as it might
no.
Curiously,
it is falling apart
Believe me
(just for once you believe in me)
it is falling apart.
To sum up then
if sum up I must
there is
a bit here
a bit there,
a bit everywhere
taken

all unaware,
I surmise,
by an urge
to improvise.
Maybe.

Now, not that I want to play things down, but I ought to explain this business to you, which is man's work and not God's, when the road ahead of one falls to pieces, crumbles, loses its way, vanishes, I don't know if you are aware of this, but it's quite possible that you are not aware of this, it's man's business, in general, losing the way. Not God's. You must have patience and let me explain. It will not take a moment. First of all you must not allow yourself to be misled by the fact that, technically speaking, it cannot be denied, this road that rolls, unrolls, and upholds, under the wheels of this carriage, effectively speaking, if we want to stick to the facts, is not falling to pieces at all. *Technically* speaking. It runs straight ahead, without hesitation, not even a bashful junction, nothing. Straight as a die. I can see that myself. But the problem, let me tell you, lies elsewhere. It is not this road, made of earth and dust and stones, that we are talking of. The road in question is another . . . And it doesn't run *outside* but *inside.* Here inside. I don't know if you recall: *my* road. Everybody has one, you know this yourself, you, besides, who are not exactly extraneous to the design of this machine that we are, all of us, each in his own way. Everybody has a road inside, a thing that simplifies, moreover, the task of this journey of ours, and only rarely complicates it. Now is one of those moments that complicate it. To sum up, then, if sum up we will, it's *that* road, the one inside, that is falling to pieces, has fallen to pieces, bless it, it can't resist anymore. It happens. Believe me. And it is not a pleasant thing.

        No.
        I believe
        it was
        O Lord Most High,
        it was
        I believe
        the sea.
        The sea
        confuses the waves
        the thoughts
        the sailing ships
        the reason suddenly commits treason
        and the roads
        that were there yesterday
        today mean nothing
        So much so that I believe
        I believe
        that that idea of yours
        of the Deluge
        was
        in fact
        A brilliant idea
        because
        if you want

to find
a punishment
I wonder
if you could find
anything better
than leaving a poor devil
alone
in the middle of that sea
Not even a beach.
Nothing.
A cliff
An abandoned wreck
Not even that.
Not a sign
to understand
which way
to go
to go to die.
So you see,
O Lord Most High,
the sea
is a kind
of small
Deluge.
Family size.
You are there,
you walk
you look
you breathe

you converse
you observe it,
from the shore, I mean,
and that one
in the meantime
takes your thoughts
of stone
that were
road
certainty
destiny
and
in exchange
offers
sails
that sway in your head
like the dance
of a woman
who will drive you
mad.
Pardon the metaphor.
But it's not easy to explain
how it is that you have no more answers
by dint of looking at the sea.

So now, to sum up, if sum up we will, the problem is this, that I have many roads around me and none inside, on the contrary, to be precise, none inside and four outside. Four. First: I go back to Elisewin and stay there with her, which was also the principal reason, if you will, for this journeying of mine. Second: I carry on this way and go to the Almayer Inn, which is not an entirely salubrious place, given its dangerous proximity to the sea, but which is also an unbelievable place, such is its beauty, and its tranquillity, and its airiness, and its anguish, and its finality. Third: I go straight on, I do not turn off toward the inn, and I go back to the Baron, in Carewall, who is waiting for me, and all things considered my home is there and there is my place. It was, at any rate. Fourth: I drop everything, take off this sad black cassock, I choose any other road, learn a trade, marry a witty woman who is not too beautiful, have a few children, grow old and finally die, with your pardon, serene and tired, like any other Christian. As you see it's not that I don't know my own mind, I know it very well but only up to a certain point in the matter. I know perfectly well what the question is. It's the answer I want.

This carriage races on, and I don't know where. I think about the answer and in my mind darkness falls

So
this darkness
I take
and I put it
in your
hands.
And I ask you
O Lord Most High
To keep it with you
For one hour only

hold it in your hand
just as long as is needed
to wash away its blackness
to wash away the ache
it gives both head,
that darkness,
and heart,
that blackness,
would you?
You could
simply
stoop
look at it
smile at it
open it
steal a light from it
and let it fall,
in any case
I'll look
to see where
it is and
find it.
A mere trifle
for you,
such a big thing
for me.
Are you listening to me
O Lord Most High?
It's not asking too much

of you
to ask if.
It's not insulting
to hope that you.
It's not foolish
to fancy that.
And then again it's only a prayer,
which is a way of writing down
the scent of an awaiting.
Write
where you will,
the way
I have lost.
A sign will do,
something,
a slight
scratch
on the glass
of these eyes
that look
without seeing,
I shall see it.
Write
on the world
just one word
written for me
I
will read it.
Lightly brush

an instant
of this silence,
I will hear it.
Do not be afraid,
I am not.

And may this prayer
slip away
with the strength of words
beyond the world's prison
to who knows where.
Amen.

A Prayer For One Who Has Once Again Found His Way, And
Therefore, to Tell the Truth, a Prayer for Me.

Have patience, do
O Lord Most High
for once again it is I

He is dying slowly,
this man
is dying slowly
as if he wished
to enjoy,
to destroy

the last life
he has.
Barons die

as do men
beyond our ken
no more.
I am here
and it's clear
that my place
was to stand here.
The dying Baron
wants news
of his daughter
no longer here
who knows where
she is
he wants to hear
she's alive
where she is
she didn't die in the sea
in the sea
she was cured.
I tell him this
and he dies
but to die this way
is a lesser death.
I talk to him
up close
and a bit slowly
and it's clear
that my place
was

here.
You took me from
a road like any other
and patiently
you brought me
to this hour
when he needed me.
And I
who was lost
in this hour
have found
myself.
It's amazing to think
you were listening
that day
really
listening
to me.
You pray
so as not to remain alone
to while away the time
you'd never dream that
God . . .
that God
likes to listen
to you.
Isn't that amazing?
You heard me
You saved me.

Of course, if I may be permitted, in all humility, I don't believe that there was really any need to cause a landslide on the Quartel road, something that was, apart from any other consideration, fairly irritating for the local folk, something milder would have been enough, probably, a more discreet sign, you know, something more intimate, between us two. The same holds true, if I may make a small objection, for the scene where the horses stopped dead—and there was absolutely no way of persuading them to continue—on the road that was taking me back to Elisewin. It was technically very well done but perhaps far too spectacular, don't you think? I would have understood even with much less, do you occasionally tend to overdo things, or am I wrong? But, be that as it may, the folk down that way are still talking about it, you don't forget a scene like that so easily. All things considered, I think that that dream of the Baron would have been enough. The one where he got up from his bed and shouted, "Father Pluche! Father Pluche!" It was a thing well done, in its way, left no room for doubt, and indeed the next morning I was already on my way to Carewall, you see it doesn't take much, at the end of the day. No, I'm telling you this, because if it should happen again, you'll know how to go about things. Dreams are the kind of stuff that works. If you want my advice, that's the best way. To save someone, if need be. A dream.

So
I shall keep
this black cassock
and these hills

lightsome hills
in my eyes
And upon me.
In saecula saeculorum
this is my place.
It's all
simpler
now.
Now
all is
simple.
I shall be able to do
what remains to do
by myself.
If you need anything,
you know where to find
Pluche,
who owes you his life.

And may this prayer
slip away
with the strength of words
beyond the world's prison
to who knows where.
Amen.

CHAPTER 3

~

Ann Deverià

Dear André, my beloved of a thousand years ago,

the little girl who has given you this letter is called Dira. I have told her to have you read it, as soon as you arrive at the inn, before letting you come up to my room. Right to the last line. Don't try to lie to her. You cannot lie to that little girl.

Sit down, then. And listen to me.

I don't know how you managed to find me. This is a place that almost does not exist. And if you ask for the Almayer Inn, people look at you in surprise, and do not know. If my husband was looking for an inaccessible corner of the world for my cure, he has found it. God knows how you managed to find it, too.

I have received your letters, and they were not easy reading. They open with pain the wounds of memory. If I had continued here, desiring and waiting for you, those letters would have been a dazzling joy. But this is a strange place. Reality fades away and everything becomes memory. Even you, little by little, ceased to be a desire and became a memory. Your letters reached me like messengers from a world that no longer exists.

I have loved you, André, and I cannot not imagine how one could love any more. I had a life, which made me happy, and I let it fall to pieces just to stay with you. I did not love you out of boredom or loneliness or caprice. I loved you because the desire for you was stronger than any happiness. And I also knew that life wasn't big enough to hold together all of desire's imaginings. But I didn't try to stop myself, or to stop you. I knew that life would have done it. And it did. Suddenly it all blew apart. There were shards everywhere and they cut like blades.

Then I came here. And this is not easy to explain. My husband thought it was a place where one might recover. But *recover* is too small a word for what happens here. And too simple. This is a place where you take leave of yourself. What you are slips away from you, bit by bit. And you leave it behind you, step by step, on this shore that does not know time and lives only one day, always the same one. The present vanishes and you become memory. You slip away from everything, fears, feelings, desires: you keep them, like cast-off clothes, in the wardrobe of an unknown wisdom, and an unhoped-for peace. Can you understand me? Can you understand how all this—is beautiful?

Believe me, it's not just a way, only an easier one, to die. I have never felt more alive than I do now. But it's different. What I am has already happened; and here, and now, it lives in me like a footprint on a trail, like a sound in an echo, and like a riddle in its answer. Not that it dies, no, not that. It slips to the other side of life. With a lightness that seems a dance.

It's a way of losing everything, in order to find everything.

If you can manage to understand all this, you will believe me when I tell you that it is impossible to think of the future. The future is an idea that has detached itself from me. It isn't important. It doesn't mean anything anymore. I have no eyes to see it with anymore. You speak of it so often, in your letters. I struggle to remember what it means. Future. Mine is already all here, and now. My future shall be the repose of a motionless time, moments collected and placed one upon the other, as if they were only one. From here to my death, there will be that moment, and that's all.

I shall not follow you, André. I shall not make any new life for myself, because I have just learned how to be the dwelling place of what has been my life. And I like it. I do not want anything else. I understand your distant islands, and I understand your dreams, your plans. But the road that can take me there no longer exists. And you cannot invent it for me, in a world that isn't there. Forgive me, my beloved, but your future will not be mine.

There is a man, in this inn, who has a funny name and studies where the sea ends. In these last few days, while I was waiting for you, I told him about us and how I was afraid of your coming and at the same time how I wanted you to come. He is a good, patient man. He sat and listened to me. And one day he said: "Write to him." He says that writing to someone is the only way to wait for him without hurting oneself. And I have written to you. I have put into this letter all I hold inside me. The man with the funny name says you will understand. He says that you will read it, then you will go out onto the beach and, walking along the seashore, you will think again about everything and you will understand. It will last an hour or a day, it doesn't matter. But in the end you will return to the inn. He says that you will climb the stairs, you will open my door, and without a word you will take me in your arms and kiss me.

I know it seems silly. But I would be glad if it really happened. Losing oneself in another's arms is a fine way to lose oneself.

Nothing can steal from me the memory of when, with all of me, I was

your Ann.

CHAPTER 4

Plasson

P ROVISIONAL CATALOG OF THE PICTORIAL WORKS OF
THE PAINTER MICHEL PLASSON, ORDERED IN CHRON-
OLOGICAL ORDER STARTING FROM THE SAID PLAS-
SON'S STAY AT THE ALMAYER INN (BY QUARTEL) UNTIL THE
DEATH OF THE SAID PLASSON.

Compiled, for the benefit of posterity, by Professor Ismael
Adelante Ismael Bartleboom, on the basis of his own personal
experience and other reliable testimony.

Dedicated to Madame Ann Deverià.

1. *Ocean sea,* oil on canvas, 15 x 21.6 cm
   The Bartleboom Collection

Description:
Completely white.

2. *Ocean sea*, oil on canvas, 80.4 x 110.5 cm
The Bartleboom Collection
Description:
Completely white.

3. *Ocean sea*, watercolor, 35 x 50.5 cm
The Bartleboom Collection
Description:
White with a vague hint of ochre on the upper part.

4. *Ocean sea*, oil on canvas, 44.2 x 100.8 cm
The Bartleboom Collection
Description:
Completely white. The signature is in red.

5. *Ocean sea*, drawing, pencil on paper, 12 x 10 cm
The Bartleboom Collection
Description:
Two dots, very close to each other, are visible in the
center of the sheet. The rest is white. (On the right-
hand margin, a stain: grease?)

6. *Ocean sea*, watercolor, 31.2 x 26 cm
The Bartleboom Collection. At present, and quite
temporarily, in the care of Mrs. Maria Luigia Severina
Hohenheith.

Description:
Completely white.
When he gave this work to me, the artist's words were,
and I quote verbatim: "It's the best I have done so far."
The tone was of profound satisfaction.

7. *Ocean sea*, oil on canvas, 120.4 x 80.5 cm
The Bartleboom Collection
Description:
Two blobs of color can be seen: one, ochre, on the upper
part of the canvas, and the other, black, on the lower
part. The rest, white. (On the back, a handwritten note:
Storm. And below: *tatatum tatatum tatatum*.)

8. *Ocean sea*, pastel on paper, 19 x 31.2 cm
The Bartleboom Collection.
Description:
In the center of the sheet, located slightly to the left, a
small blue sail. The rest, white.

9. *Ocean sea*, oil on canvas, 340.8 x 220.5 cm
The Quartel District Museum. Catalog number: 87
Description:
On the right, a dark cliff emerges from the water. Very
high waves, breaking against the rocks, foam
spectacularly. Amid the storm, two ships can be seen as
they succumb to the sea. Four longboats are suspended
on the edge of a whirlpool. The shipwrecked are packed
aboard the longboats. Some of them, having fallen into

the sea, are going under. But this is a high sea, much higher down there toward the horizon than it is close by, and it hides the horizon from view, against all logic, it seems to be rising as if the whole world were rising and we were sinking, here where we are, in the womb of the earth, while an ever more majestic comber looms over us and, horrified, the night falls on this monster. (Dubious attribution. Almost certainly a forgery.)

10. *Ocean sea*, watercolor, 20.8 x 16 cm
    The Bartleboom Collection
    Description:
    Completely white.

11. *Ocean sea*, oil on canvas, 66.7 x 81 cm
    The Bartleboom Collection
    Description:
    Completely white. (Badly damaged. Probably fallen in water.)

12. *Portrait of Ismael Adelante Ismael Bartleboom*, pencil on paper, 41.5 x 41.5 cm
    Description:
    Completely white. In the center, in italic script, the word *Bartleb*

13. *Ocean sea*, oil on canvas, 46.2 x 51.9 cm
    The Bartleboom Collection
    Description:

Completely white. In this case, however, the expression should be understood literally: the canvas is completely covered by thick brushstrokes of white paint.

14. *At the Almayer Inn*, oil on canvas, 50 x 42 cm
    The Bartleboom Collection
    Description:
    A portrait of an angel in the Pre-Raphaelite manner.
    The face is devoid of lineaments. The wings display a
    meaningful richness of color. Gold background.

15. *Ocean sea*, watercolor, 118 x 80.6 cm
    The Bartleboom Collection
    Description:
    Three small blobs of blue paint on the top left (sails?).
    The rest, white. On the back, a handwritten note: *Pajamas
    and socks.*

16. *Ocean sea*, pencil on paper, 28 x 31.7 cm
    The Bartleboom Collection
    Description:
    Eighteen sails, of diverse dimensions, scattered about
    without any precise order. In the lower left-hand corner,
    a small sketch of a three-master, clearly the work of
    another hand, probably that of a child (Dol?).

17. *Portrait of Madame Ann Deverià*, oil on canvas, 52.8 x 30 cm
    The Bartleboom Collection
    Description:

A woman's hand of the palest color, the fingers marvelously tapering. White background.

18, 19, 20, 21. *Ocean sea*, pencil on paper, 12 x 12 cm
The Bartleboom Collection
Description:
A series of four sketches, all apparently absolutely identical. A simple horizontal line crosses them from left to right (but also from right to left, if you will) more or less midway up the canvas. In reality, Plasson maintained that these were four profoundly different images. He said, and I quote, "They are four profoundly different images." My own highly personal impression is that they represent the same view at four successive different times of the day. When I expressed this opinion of mine to the artist, he occasioned to reply, and I quote verbatim, "Do you think so?"

22. Untitled, pencil on paper, 20.8 x 13.5 cm
The Bartleboom Collection
Description:
A young man, on the shore, draws near the sea, carrying in his arms the abandoned body of an unclothed woman. Moon in the sky and reflections on the water. In consideration of the time that has now passed since the dramatic events with which it is connected, I am now making public this sketch, long kept secret by the artist's express wish.

23. *Ocean sea*, oil on canvas, 71.6 x 38.4 cm
    The Bartleboom Collection
    Description:
    A deep dark red slash cuts the canvas from left to right.
    The rest, white.

24. *Ocean sea*, oil on canvas, 127 x 108.6 cm
    The Bartleboom Collection
    Description:
    Completely white. This is the last work executed during
    the stay at the Almayer Inn, by Quartel. The artist
    presented it to the inn, expressing the wish that it might
    be shown on a wall facing the sea. Subsequently, and
    through channels that I have never quite managed to
    determine, it came into my possession. I am looking
    after it, keeping it at the disposal of anyone able to
    claim ownership.

25, 26, 27, 28, 29, 30, 31, 32. Untitled, oil on canvas, various
    dimensions
    The Museum of St. Jacques de Grance
    Description:
    Eight portraits of sailors, stylistically traceable to
    Plasson in his early manner. Abbot Ferrand, who was
    kind enough to inform me of their existence, affirms
    that the artist executed them gratis, as a token of his
    affection for some people with whom he had struck up a
    sincere friendship during his stay at St. Jacques. With

engaging candor, the abbot confessed to me that he had asked the painter if he might have his portrait painted by him, but had met with a firm yet courteous refusal. It seems that the exact words pronounced by Plasson in the circumstances were, "Unfortunately you are not a sailor, and therefore your face has no sea in it. You see, these days I only know how to paint the sea."

33. *Ocean sea*, oil on canvas (dimensions uncertain) (Lost)
Description:
Completely white. Here, too, Abbot Ferrand provided extremely valuable testimony. He had the frankness to admit that, owing to an inexplicable misunderstanding, the canvas, found in the painter's lodgings the day following his departure, had been considered a simple blank canvas and not a completed work of considerable value. As such, it was carried off by persons unknown and has not been found to this day.

34, 35, 36. Untitled, oil on canvas, 68.8 x 82 cm
The Gallen-Martendorf Museum, Helleborg
Description:
These are three very accurate, almost identical, copies of a painting by Hans van Dyke, *The Harbor at Skalen*. The Gallen-Martendorf Museum has cataloged them as works by van Dyke himself, thus perpetrating a deplorable misunderstanding. As I have many times

pointed out to the curator of the abovementioned museum, Prof. Broderfons, the three canvases not only bear on the back the clear annotation "van Plasson," but also display a detail that makes Plasson's authorship evident: in all three the painter depicted at work on the harbor mole, at the bottom left, has an easel in front of him bearing a completely white canvas. In the original by van Dyke, the canvas is painted normally. Professor Broderfons, while admitting the correctness of my observation, accounts it of no particular significance. Professor Broderfons is, besides, an incompetent scholar and an absolutely unbearable man.

37. *Lake Constance*, watercolor, 27 x 31.9 cm
The Bartleboom Collection
Description:
A painting of accurate and very elegant execution, portraying the celebrated Lake Constance at sunset. The colors are warm and smoky. No human figures appear. But the water and the shores are rendered with great poetry and intensity. Plasson sent me this canvas accompanied by a brief note, the text of which I report here verbatim: "It's weariness, my friend, Beautiful weariness. Adieu."

38. *Ocean sea*, pencil on paper, 26 x 13.4 cm
The Bartleboom Collection
Description:

The drawing depicts, with accuracy and precision,
Plasson's left hand. Plasson, I am obliged to add, was
left-handed.

39. *Ocean sea*, pencil on paper, 26 x 13.4 cm
The Bartleboom Collection
Description:
Plasson's left hand. Without shading.

40. *Ocean sea*, pencil on paper, 26 x 13.4 cm
The Bartleboom Collection
Description:
Plasson's left hand. Few lines, barely sketched in.

41. *Ocean sea*, pencil on paper, 26 x 13.4 cm
The Bartleboom Collection
Description:
Plasson's left hand. Three lines and some light shading.
Note: This drawing was presented to me, along with the
three preceding works, by Dr. Monnier, the doctor who
looked after Plasson during the brief and painful course
of his last illness (pneumonia). According to his
testimony, which I have no reason to doubt, these were
the last four works by Plasson, bedridden by that time
and getting weaker every day. Still, according to the same
witness, Plasson died in serene solitude and with his soul
in peace. A few minutes before expiring, he uttered the
following phrase: "It's not a question of colors, it's a

question of music, do you understand? It took me such a long time, but now" (stop)

He was a generous man and certainly one gifted with an enormous artistic talent. He was my friend. And I loved him.

Now he is at rest, by his express wish, in the cemetery of Quartel. The tombstone, over his grave, is in simple stone. Completely white.

CHAPTER 5

~

Bartleboom

I T WENT LIKE THIS. He had gone to take the waters, Bartleboom, at the spa of Bad Hollen, a frightful place, if you see what I mean. He used to go there for certain complaints that bothered him, to do with his prostate, an annoying business, a nuisance. When it gets you down there it's a real nuisance, always, nothing serious, mind, but you have to take care, you have to do loads of ridiculous, humiliating things. As for him, Bartleboom always used to go to the spa at Bad Hollen, for example. A frightful place, among other things.

But anyway.

Bartleboom was there with his fiancée, a certain Maria Luigia Severina Hohenheith, a beautiful woman, there was no doubt, but of the opera-house variety, if you see what I mean.

All front. You felt like turning her around to see if there was anything behind the makeup and the gush and all the rest. You didn't do it of course, but you felt like it. Bartleboom, to tell the truth, had not pledged his troth with much enthusiasm; on the contrary. This should be said. One of his aunts, Aunt Matilda, had done everything. You have to understand that at that time he was virtually surrounded by aunts, and to tell the whole story, he *depended* on them, economically I mean, he didn't have two pennies to rub together. It was the aunts who paid up. Which was the exact consequence of that impassioned and total dedication to science that had bound Bartleboom's life to that ambitious *Encyclopedia of the Limits* etcetera, a great and meritorious work, which, however, prevented him, obviously, from attending to his professional duties, persuading him every year to leave his position as professor and his corresponding salary to a temporary substitute, who in this case—that is, throughout the entire seventeen-year period in which this state of affairs continued—was me. From this, as you will understand, springs my gratitude to him, and my admiration for his work. It goes without saying. These are things that a man of honor does not forget.

But anyway.

Aunt Matilda had done everything, and Bartleboom hadn't been able to put up much in the way of resistance. He was betrothed. But he hadn't taken it particularly well. He had lost some of that sparkle . . . his soul had clouded over, if you see what I mean. It was as if he had expected something different, something quite different. He wasn't prepared for all that normality. He soldiered on, no more than that. Then one day, there in Bad Hollen, he and his fiancée and his prostate went to a reception, an elegant affair, all champagne and gay popular music. Waltzes. And there he met Anna Ancher. She was special, that woman. She painted. And well, too, they said. Another type altogether, compared to Maria Luigia Severina, you understand. It was she who stopped him, amid the hubbub of the party.

"Excuse me . . . you are Professor Bartleboom, aren't you?"

"Yes."

"I am a friend of Michel Plasson's."

It emerged that the painter had written to her thousands of times, telling her about Bartleboom and other things, and in particular about that *Encyclopedia of the Limits* etcetera, an account that, according to her, had made quite an impression on her.

"I would be charmed to see your work one day."

That's exactly what she said: *charmed.* She said it tilting her little head slightly to one side and pushing back a lock of raven hair from her eyes. Masterly stuff. For Bartleboom it was as if those words had been injected directly into his bloodstream. They reverberated all the way down to his trousers, so to speak. He mumbled something and from then on he did nothing but sweat. He sweated brilliantly, he did, when he needed to. The temperature had nothing to do with it. He did it all by himself.

Perhaps it might have all ended there, that story, but the next day, when he was out walking, alone, turning those words and all the rest over and over in his head, Bartleboom saw a carriage going past, one of those handsome ones, with luggage and hatboxes on the top. It was heading out of town. And inside, he could see her perfectly, was Anna Ancher. It was really her. Raven hair. Little head. The lot. Even the reverberations in the trousers were the same as the day before. Bartleboom understood. Despite what they say around town, he was a man who, when it was necessary, was capable of taking his decisions and no mistake, when it was necessary he didn't hang back. And so he went back home, packed his bags, and, all ready to leave, presented himself before his fiancée, Maria Luigia Severina. She was busy amid a muddle of brushes, ribbons, and necklaces.

"Maria Luigia . . ."

"Please, Ismael, I am already late . . ."

"Maria Luigia, I wish to inform you that you are no longer betrothed."

"Very well, Ismael, we shall discuss it later."

"And as a consequence, I am no longer betrothed either."

"That's obvious, Ismael."

"Good-bye, then."

What was amazing about that woman was the slowness of her reactions. We talked about the matter more than once with Bartleboom. He was absolutely fascinated by that phenomenon, he had also studied it, so to speak, and had ended up by acquiring a virtually scientific and complete competence in the subject. In the circumstances, he was therefore perfectly aware that the time at his disposal to get away from that house scot-free was between twenty-two and twenty-six seconds. He had calculated that this would have been enough for him to reach the coach. And in fact it was in the precise moment that he was lowering his bottom onto the seat of the conveyance that the clear morning air of Bad Hollen was shattered by an inhuman scream:

"BAAAAAAARTLEBOOM!"

What a voice she had, that woman. Even years afterwards, in Bad Hollen, they said that it was as if someone had dropped a piano straight onto a warehouse full of crystal chandeliers.

Bartleboom had made his inquiries: the Anchers stayed at Hollenberg, fifty-four miles north of Bad Hollen. He set off. He was wearing his Sunday best. Even his hat was his Sunday hat. He was sweating, true, but within the limits of common decency. The coach bowled along the road between the hills. Everything seemed to be going in the best way possible.

Bartleboom was quite clear about the words he would say to Anna Ancher, when he appeared before her:

"Miss Ancher, I have been waiting for you. I have been waiting for you for years."

And, bingo, he would hand her the mahogany box with all the letters, hundreds of letters, a sight that would leave her dumbfounded with amazement and tenderness. It was a good plan, no mistake. Bartleboom ran through it over and over again during the journey, and this provides food for thought on the complexity of the minds of certain great scholars and thinkers—as was Professor Bartleboom, beyond any shadow of a doubt—to whom the sublime faculty of concentrating on an idea with abnormal perspicacity and profundity has the questionable corollary of removing instantly, and in a singularly complete fashion, all other neighboring, related, and associated ideas. Mad as hatters, in short. So, for example, Bartleboom spent the whole journey verifying the unassailable logic of his plan, but only seven miles outside Hollenberg, and specifically between the villages of Alzen and Balzen, he remembered, to be precise, that that mahogany box, and therefore all the letters, hundreds of letters, *was no longer in his possession.*

Things like that come as a real blow. If you see what I mean.

As a matter of fact, Bartleboom had given the box with the letters to Maria Luigia Severina, on the day of their betrothal. Without much conviction, he had nonetheless brought her the lot, with a certain solemnity, saying, "I have been waiting for you. I have been waiting for you for years."

After those ten, twelve seconds of the customary hiatus, Maria Luigia had rolled her eyes, arched her neck, and, incredulous, had proffered a single elementary word:

"Me?"

"Me?" was not exactly the response that Bartleboom had been dreaming of for years, while he was writing those letters and living on his own, getting by the best he could. And so it goes without saying that he was left a little disappointed in the circumstances, as you can understand. This also explains why, later, he never brought up the matter of the letters again, limiting himself to checking that the mahogany box was still there, at Maria Luigia's, and God only knew if anyone had ever opened it. It happens. You have your dreams, personal stuff, intimate, and then life decides it doesn't want to play along, and it dismantles them, a moment, a few words, and everything falls apart. It happens. That's why life is such a wretched business. You have to resign yourself. Life has no *gratitude,* if you see what I mean.

Gratitude.

But anyway.

Now the problem was that he needed the box, but it was in one of the worst possible places, that is to say somewhere in Maria Luigia's house. Bartleboom got off the coach at Balzen, five miles outside Hollenberg, spent the night at the inn, and the next morning took the coach going in the other direction, back to Bad Hollen. His odyssey had begun, if you can believe me.

He adopted the usual technique with Maria Luigia; it could not fail. He presented himself unannounced in the room where she was languishing in bed, getting over her nervous prostration, and without preamble said, "I have come to take the letters, dear."

"They are on the desk, my treasure," she replied with a certain tenderness. Then, after exactly twenty-six seconds, she emitted a strangulated groan and fainted. Bartleboom, it goes without saying, was already long gone.

He took the coach again, this time in the direction of Hollenberg, and on the evening of the next day he presented himself at the Ancher residence. They accompanied him into the drawing-room, where he very nearly dropped dead, stone dead in his tracks. The young lady was at the piano, and she was playing—with her little head, the raven hair, and all the rest—

playing like an angel. Alone there, she and the piano and that was all. Unbelievable. Bartleboom stood as if turned to stone, with his mahogany box in his hand, on the threshold of the drawing room, completely besotted. He couldn't even manage to sweat. All he could do was stare.

When the music finished, the young lady looked toward him. Definitively ravished, he crossed the drawing room, stood before her, placed the mahogany box on the piano, and said, "Miss Anna, I have been waiting for you. I have been waiting for you for years."

Once again the response was a singular one:

"I'm not Anna."

"Begging your pardon?"

"My name is Elisabetta. Anna is my sister."

Twins, if you see what I mean.

Like two peas in a pod.

"My sister is at Bad Hollen, at the spa. About fifty miles from here."

"Yes, I know the road, thank you."

Things like that come as a blow. And no mistake. A real blow. Fortunately Bartleboom had resources, he had real spiritual staying power, in that carcass of his. He took to the road again, destination Bad Hollen. If that was where Anna Ancher was, that was where he had to go. Simple. He was more or less halfway there when things began to strike him as being a little less simple. The fact is, he couldn't manage to get that music out of his head. Or the piano, the hands on the keyboard, the little head with the raven hair, the whole vision, in other words. Stuff so perfect that it seemed the devil's work. Or the work of fate, said Bartleboom to himself. The Professor began to suffer over this story of the twins, both the pianist and the painter, he couldn't make head or tail of anything anymore, it was understandable. The more time passed, the less he understood. You might say that for every mile of road, he understood a mile less. He got off at Pozel, six miles out of Bad Hollen. And there he spent the night. The next day he took the coach for Hollenberg: he had opted for the pianist. More attractive, he thought. He changed his mind on the twenty-second mile: at Bazel, to be precise, where he got off and spent the night. He left again early the next morning with the coach for Bad Hollen—already intimately betrothed to Anna Ancher, the painter—only to stop at Suzer, a little town two miles from Pozel, where he definitively established that, as far as character was concerned, he was cut out more for Elisabetta, the pianist. In the days that followed, his oscillatory movements took him once more to Alzen, then to Tozer, from there to Balzen, and then back again as far as Fazel, and thence, in order, to Palzen, Rulzen, Alzen (for the third time), and Colzen. By that time the local folk were convinced that he was an inspector from some ministry. Everybody treated him very well. At Alzen, the third time he passed through, he even found a reception committee waiting for him. He took but little account of this. He wasn't a formal type. He was a simple man, was Bartleboom, one hell of a simple man. And a fair one. Really.

But anyway.

That business could not go on forever. Even though the citizenry appeared well disposed. Sooner or later it had to stop. Bartleboom understood this. And after twelve days of passionate oscillation, he dressed suitably for the occasion and headed straight for Bad Hollen. He had decided: he would live with a painter. He arrived on a Sunday evening. Anna Ancher was not at home. She would be back shortly. "I'll wait," he said. And he took a seat in a sitting room. It was there that a simple and ruinous image suddenly came to mind with the force of a lightning bolt: his mahogany box, all nice and shiny, sitting on the piano in the Anchers' house. He had forgotten it there. These are things that normal people find hard to understand, me for example, because it's part of the mystery of great minds, it's their specialty, the mechanisms of genius, capable of magnificent acrobatics and colossal screw-ups. Bartleboom was one of that species. Colossal screw-ups, sometimes. But he did not get flustered. He got to his feet and, leaving a message that he would return later, repaired to a little hotel outside town. The next day he took the coach for Hollenberg. He was beginning to get to know that road rather well, he was becoming, so to speak, a real expert on it. If ever they had instituted a university chair for studies on that road, you could bet that it would have been his, guaranteed.

At Hollenberg things went off smoothly. The box was indeed there.

"I would have sent it to you, but I had absolutely no idea where to find you," said Elisabetta Ancher with a voice that would have seduced a deaf man. Bartleboom vacillated for a moment, but then he recovered.

"It doesn't matter, it's perfectly all right this way."

He kissed her hand and took his leave. He didn't sleep a

wink all night long, but the next morning he showed up punctually for the Bad Hollen coach. A fine trip. At every stop he was greeted and made much of. The folk were becoming fond of him. They are like that, in those parts, sociable folk, they don't ask too many questions and they treat you with complete sincerity. Really. A frightfully unattractive area, this has to be said, but the people are exquisite. The kind they don't make anymore.

But anyway.

Finally, Bartleboom arrived in Bad Hollen with his mahogany box, the letters and everything. He went back to Anna Ancher's house and had himself announced. The painter was working on a still life, apples pears pheasants, things like that; the pheasants kept still of course, but then again they were dead and it was a still life after all. She held her little head slightly tilted to one side. Her raven hair framed her face charmingly. Had there been a piano, too, you wouldn't have doubted that it was the other one, the Hollenberg one. But it was her, the Bad Hollen one. Peas in a pod, I say. It's prodigious what nature can manage to do when it gets to work with a will. Unbelievable. Really.

"Professor Bartleboom, what a surprise!" she twittered.

"Good day, Miss Ancher," he replied, adding immediately, "It is *Anna* Ancher, isn't it?"

"Yes, why?"

He wanted to be on the safe side, did the Professor. You never know.

"What has brought you all this way, to delight me with your visit?"

"This," replied Bartleboom seriously, placing the mahogany box in front of her and opening it before her eyes.

"I have been waiting for you, Anna. I have been waiting for you for years."

The painter reached out and rapidly shut the box again.

"Before our conversation goes any further, I ought to inform you of something, Professor Bartleboom."

"Whatever you wish, my beloved."

"I am betrothed."

"Really?"

"I became engaged six days ago to Lieutenant Gallega."

"An excellent choice."

"Thank you."

Bartleboom mentally worked his way back to six days before. It had been the day on which, having arrived from Rulzen, he had stopped at Colzen before setting off again for Alzen. Right in the middle of his tribulations, in short. Six days. Six wretched days. By the way, that Gallega was a real parasite, if you see what I mean, an insignificant creature and in a certain sense even a noxious one. It was mortifying. Really. Mortifying.

"Now, do you wish us to continue?"

"I no longer think that that will be necessary," replied Bartleboom, taking back his mahogany box.

On the way back to his hotel, the Professor attempted a cold analysis of the situation and he came to the conclusion that there were two possibilities (a circumstance, it will be noted, that occurs with a certain frequency, the possibilities being generally two and only rarely three): either this was merely a disagreeable hitch, in which case what he had to do was to challenge the abovementioned Lieutenant Gallega to a duel and get rid of him. Or it was a clear sign of destiny, a magnanimous destiny, and in that case what he had to do was return as fast as possible to Hollenberg and marry Elisabetta Ancher, the unforgotten pianist.

By the way, Bartleboom hated duels. He just could not bear them.

"Dead pheasants . . ." he thought with a certain disgust. And he decided to leave. Seated in his place aboard the first coach of the morning, he took the road for Hollenberg once more. He was in serene mood and accepted with benevolent good nature the manifestations of cheerful affection accorded him by the populations of the towns of Pozel, Colzen, Tozer, Rulzen, Palzen, Alzen, Balzen, and Fazel. Likable folk, as I have said. At dusk he presented himself, impeccably dressed and holding his mahogany box, at the Anchers' house.

"Miss Elisabetta, please," he said with a certain solemnity to the servant who opened the door.

"She isn't in, sir. She left this morning for Bad Hollen."

Unbelievable.

A man of another moral and cultural background would have perhaps retraced his steps and taken the first coach for Bad Hollen. A man of lesser psychic and nervous fiber perhaps would have given himself over to the most theatrical expressions of a definitive and incurable discouragement. But Bartleboom was an upright and just man, one of those who have a certain style when it comes to digesting the whims of destiny.

Bartleboom began to laugh.

But heartily, really splitting his sides, enough to triple himself up with laughter, there was no way to stop him, with tears and everything, a sight to see, a chaotic, oceanic, apocalyptic laugh, an endless laugh. The Anchers' servants no longer knew what to do, there was no way to make him stop, neither cajolery nor threats had any effect, he just carried on laughing fit to burst, an embarrassing business, and infectious apart from anything else, you know how it is, one starts and the rest follow, it's the law of the giggles, it's like a plague, you want to try to keep a straight face, you can't manage, it's inexorable, nothing can be done, they were collapsing one by one, the servants, despite the fact they had nothing to laugh about, on the contrary, to be precise, they ought to have been worried about that embarrassing if not exactly dramatic situation, but they were collapsing one by one, laughing their heads off, you could have wet yourself, if you see what I mean, wet yourself, if you weren't careful. In the end they put him to bed. He also laughed from a horizontal position, however, and with such enthusiasm, with such generosity, a prodigy, really, what with sobs tears and choking, but unstoppable, prodigious, really. One and a half hours later he was still there laughing. And he hadn't stopped for a second. By that time the servants were at their wits' end, they were running out of the house so as to avoid hearing any more of that exhilarating and infectious sobbing laughter, they tried to escape, their guts writhing with the pain of all that gargantuan guffawing, they were trying to save themselves, and you can easily understand them, by that time it was becoming a question of life and death. Unbelievable. Then, at a certain point, Bartleboom stopped without warning; like a mechanism that had jammed, he suddenly became serious again, looked around, and having identified the nearest servant within range, he said, very seriously, "Have you seen a mahogany box?"

The servant jumped at the chance to make himself useful, as long as he stopped laughing.

"Here it is, sir."

"Well, it's a present for you," said Bartleboom, and off he went again, laughing his head off, as if he had come out with some irresistible witticism, the best one of his life, the biggest, so to speak, a major witticism. From then on he didn't stop.

He spent the whole night laughing. Apart from the Anchers' servants, who were walking about with cotton wool in their ears by that time, it was a nuisance for the whole of peaceful Hollenberg, since Bartleboom's laughter, you see, overspilled the confines of the house proper and spread marvelously through that nocturnal silence. Sleep was out of the question. It was already something if you managed to stay serious. And at first, as a matter of fact, you could stay serious, also in view of the irritation aroused by that vexatious racket, but common sense went to pot very soon, and the germ of the giggles began to spread, unstoppable, to devour everybody, without distinction, men and women, not to mention the children, really everybody. Like an epidemic. There were houses in which no one had laughed for months, they didn't even remember how it was done. People sunk deep in their own rancor and wretchedness. Not the luxury of a smile, for months. And that night, everyone set to laughing, laughing fit to bust a gut, it was unheard of, they could barely recognize one another, the mask of those eternal long faces of theirs had fallen away to reveal a gaping smirk. A revelation. It was enough to make you rediscover your *joie de vivre* to see the lights of that little town coming on again one by one, to hear the houses come down with gusts of laughter, without there being anything to laugh about, but just like that, miraculously, as if on that very night the barrel of collective and unanimous patience had brimmed over, and—here's to all misery!—had flooded the entire town with a roaring torrent of blessed mirth. A concert that touched the heart. A wonder. Bartleboom himself was conducting the choir. It was his moment, so to speak. And he was conducting it like a real maestro. A memorable night, I tell you. Ask, by all means. Damned if it wasn't a memorable night.

But anyway.

At the first light of dawn, he calmed down. Bartleboom, I mean. And then the whole town gradually followed suit. They stopped laughing, little by little, and then definitively. It went as it had come. Bartleboom asked for something to eat. Understandably, his exploit had left him with an enormous appetite, it's no joke laughing for all that time, and with all that enthusiasm. But as far as health was concerned, he looked very much as if he had plenty and to spare.

"Never felt better," he assured the delegation of citizens that, to a certain extent out of gratitude and in any case out of curiosity, had come to see how he was. He had made some new friends. There was no doubt that he was fated to end up making friends with the people of that area. Really. In any case he got up, said good-bye to everybody, and prepared to depart once more. His mind was made up as far as that was concerned.

"Which is the road to the capital?"

"You should go back to Bad Hollen, sir, and from there take . . ."

"Out of the question," and he left in the opposite direction, aboard a gig belonging to a neighbor, a blacksmith and a talent in his field, a real talent. He had spent the night killing himself laughing. In short, he owed a debt of gratitude, so to speak. He closed his smithy that day and took Bartleboom away from those places, and from those memories, and from everything, to blazes with it, he would never come back, the Professor, it was over, that story, for good or for ill, it was over, once and for all, Good Christ Almighty. Over.

Just like that.

After that, Bartleboom didn't try again. To get married, that is. He said that the time had passed, and that there was no more to be said. I think that he suffered a bit on account of that, but he didn't burden you with it, he kept his sorrows to himself, and could ignore them. He was one of those men who, in any case, have a cheerful view of life. A man at peace with himself, if you see what I mean. In the seven years he lived here, below us, it was always a pleasure to have him here, below us, and many times in our house, as if he were one of the family, and in a certain sense he really was. Apart from anything else, he could have lived in a very different part of town, he could, with all that money that came to him in recent years, inheritances, you understand, the aunts were dropping one after another, like ripe apples, may they rest in peace, a regular procession of notaries, one testament after another, willy-nilly, they all brought cash into Bartleboom's pocket. In short, had he wanted to, he could have lived in another part of town altogether. But he stayed here. He used to say that you lived well, in our part of town. He knew how to appreciate things, so to speak. These things too, are the measure of a man.

He continued working on that *Encyclopedia of the Limits* etcetera right up to the end. Lately he had begun to rewrite it. He used to say that science was making giant strides and that the need to bring things up to date, to specify, correct, and polish, was never-ending. He was fascinated by the idea that an *Encyclopedia of Limits* should end up becoming a book that never ended. An infinite book. It was a fine absurdity, if you think about it, and he would laugh about it, he would explain it to me over and over again, amazed, even amused. Another man perhaps would have suffered. But he, as I say, wasn't cut out for certain tribulations. He was cheerful, that one.

Needless to say, even dying was a thing that he accomplished in his own way. Without too much show, understated. He took to his bed one day, he wasn't very well, and by the following week it was all over. It was hard to understand whether he suffered or not, in those days, I asked him, but all that mattered to him was that that trifling business didn't make any of us sad. Putting people out irked him. Only once he asked me if I would please hang up one of those paintings by his painter friend on the wall in front of the bed. That was another unbelievable story, the one about the collection of Plassons.

Almost all white, if you can believe me. But he cared very much for them. Even the one that I hung up, that time, was quite white, all white, he had chosen it from the whole collection, and I hung it up there for him, so he could see it well from the bed. It was white, I swear. But he would look at it, and look at it again, he turned it over and over in his eyes, so to speak.

"The sea," he would say softly.

He died in the morning. He closed his eyes and didn't open them again. Simple.

I don't know. There are people who die and, with all due respect, you don't lose anything. But he was one of those that when they're gone you feel it. As if the whole world had become, from one day to the next, a little heavier. Could be that this planet, and the whole thing, stays afloat in the air only because there are plenty of Bartlebooms around to hold it up. With that buoyancy of theirs. They don't look like heroes, but in the meantime they keep the show on the road. They're made like that. Bartleboom was made like that. For example, he was capable of taking you by the arm, on a day like any other, in the street, and saying to you, in great secrecy, "Once I saw the angels. They were on the seashore."

Even though he didn't believe in God, he was a scientist, and had no great religious leanings, if you see what I mean. But he had seen the angels. And he would tell you about it. He would take you by the arm, on a day like any other, in the street and with wonder in his eyes, he would tell you about it.

"Once I saw the angels."

How can you not love a man like that?

CHAPTER 6

Savigny

"Y OU ARE LEAVING US then, Dr. Savigny . . ."

"Yes, sir."

"And you have decided to return to France."

"Yes."

"It will not be easy for you . . . I mean, people's curiosity, the gazettes, the politicians . . . I fear that a real hunt is on for the survivors of that raft . . ."

"They have told me."

"It has almost became a matter of state. It happens, when politics comes into it . . ."

"Sooner or later, you'll see, they will all forget this story."

"I don't doubt it, my dear Savigny. Here: these are your embarkation papers."

"I owe you a great deal, Captain."

"Don't mention it."

"And as for your doctor, perhaps I owe him my life . . . he has worked miracles."

"Savigny, if we start counting the miracles in this story, we will never finish. Go. And good luck."

"Thank you, Captain . . . Oh, one more thing."

"Yes?"

"That . . . that helmsman . . . Thomas . . . they say he escaped from the hospital . . ."

"Yes, it's a strange story. Of course it would not have happened here, but there, in the civilian hospital, you can well imagine how . . ."

"Nothing more has been heard of him?"

"No, for the moment, no. But he cannot have gone very far, in his condition. Most likely he is dead, somewhere or other . . ."

"Dead?"

"Well, it's the least one may think of one who . . . Oh, forgive me: was he perhaps a friend of yours?"

"IT WILL NOT BE DIFFICULT, Savigny, you only have to repeat what you have written in those memoirs of yours. While we're on the subject you must have made a pretty penny, eh, with that little book . . . people are reading nothing else in the salons . . ."

"I asked you if it was really necessary for me to appear in court."

"Oh no it wouldn't be necessary, but this is a devil of a trial, the eyes of the whole country are on us, we can't work properly . . . everything done by the strict letter of the law, absurd . . ."

"Chaumareys will be there, too . . ."

"Of course he will . . . he wants to defend himself, that one . . . he has no chance, none, the people want his head and they'll have it."

"It wasn't his fault alone."

"That counts for nothing, Savigny. He was the captain. He was the one who brought the *Alliance* to that sandbank, he was the one who decided to abandon her, and, just to finish things off with a flourish, he was the one who set you adrift on that infernal trap . . ."

"Very well, very well, forget it. We'll be seeing each other in court."

"Just one more thing . . ."

"Let me go, Parpeil."

"*Maître* Parpeil, if you please."

"Good-bye."

"No, you cannot go."

"What now?"

"Oh, a bore . . . a mere trifle, but, you know, it's better to be careful . . . there's a rumor going around, it seems that someone has written a . . . let's call it a diary, a kind of diary of those days on the raft . . . it seems that this person is a sailor and this already says a lot about the importance of this matter . . . fancy a sailor who *writes*, an absurdity, obviously, but in any case it seems that one of the survivors . . ."

"Thomas. Thomas could write."

"Pardon me?"

"No, nothing."

"Well, anyhow, it seems that in this diary there are things . . . in a certain sense . . . embarrassing, let's say . . . in other words, the tale is a little different from the way you and the others have told it . . ."

"And he read. Books. He could read and write."

"By God, will you listen to me?"

"Yes?"

"Try to understand, it takes nothing to cook up a thoroughgoing libel . . . it could even ruin you . . . well I was wondering, if need be, if you would be prepared to utilize a certain sum of money, you understand me, there is no other way to defend yourself from libel, and besides it's better to cover up the matter before . . . Savigny! Where the devil are you going? Savigny! Look, there's no need whatsoever to take offense, I was telling you for your own good, I know my job . . ."

"YOUR TESTIMONY HAS BEEN extremely valuable, Dr. Savigny. The court thanks you. You may step down."

". . ."

"Dr. Savigny . . ."

"Yes, excuse me, I wanted . . ."

"Have you something to add?"

"No . . . or rather . . . only one thing . . . I wanted to say

218

that . . . the sea, the sea is different . . . you cannot judge what happens in there . . . the sea is another thing."

"Doctor, this is a tribunal of the Royal Navy: the court knows perfectly well what the sea is."

"Do you think so?"

"BELIEVE ME, reading this exquisite little book of yours was such a thrill . . . even too much of a thrill for an old lady like me . . ."

"Madame la Marquise, what are you saying . . ."

"It's the truth, Dr. Savigny, that book is so . . . how can I say . . . realistic, that's it, I was reading it and I felt as if I were there on that raft, in the middle of the sea, it gave me the shivers . . ."

"You flatter me, Madame la Marquise."

"No, no . . . that book is really . . ."

"Good day, Dr. Savigny."

"Adele . . ."

"Adele, daughter of mine, one does not keep a man as busy as the doctor waiting for such a long time . . ."

"Oh, I'm sure you will have tormented him with a thousand questions about his adventures, is it not so, Savigny?"

"It is a pleasure conversing with your mother."

"A little longer and even the tea would have gone cold."

"You look splendid, Adele."

"Thank you."

"Another cup, Doctor?"

"DID HE HAVE dark eyes?"

"Yes."

"Tall, with black hair, straight . . ."

"Tied up at the nape of the neck, sir."

"A sailor?"

"He could have been. But he was dressed . . . normally, almost elegantly."

"And he did not say his name."

"No. He only said he would return."

"That he would return?"

"WE FOUND HIM at an inn on the river . . . pure chance . . . we were looking for two deserters, and we found him . . . he says his name is Philippe."

"And he did not try to escape?"

"No. He protested, he wanted to know why on earth we were taking him away . . . the usual stuff. This way, Savigny."

"And you, what did you say to him?"

"Nothing. The police are not obliged to explain when they put someone in jail these days. Of course, we won't be able to hold him for long unless we find a good reason . . . but you will see to that, won't you?"

"Of course."

"Right, then, come. No, do not lean out too far. He's there, do you see him? The second last in the row."

"The one leaning against the wall . . ."

"Yes. Is it him?"

"I'm afraid not."

"No?"

"No, I'm sorry."

"But the description, he fits it perfectly."

"Perfectly, yes, but it is not him."

"Savigny . . . now listen to me . . . you may well be a hero of the Realm, you may also be a friend of all the ministers in the world, but that one down there is already the fourth that . . ."

"It does not matter. You have already done a great deal."

"No, listen to me. We shall never find him, that man, and do you know why? Because that man is dead. He escaped from some lousy hospital in some stinking corner of Africa, he managed a few miles in some infernal desert and there he got himself roasted by the sun until he croaked. *C'est fini.* That man, now, is on the other side of the world, busy fertilizing a heap of sand."

"That man, now, is in this city, and is about to reach me. Look here."

"A letter?"

"Two days ago somebody left it in front of my door. Read it, read it by all means . . ."

"Only one word . . . ?"

"But a very clear one, don't you think?"

"*Thomas* . . ."

"Thomas. You are right, Pastor. You will never find that

man. But not because he is dead. Because he is *alive*. He is more alive than both of us put together. He is as alive as an animal stalking its prey."

"Savigny, I assure you that . . ."

"He is alive. And, unlike me, he has an excellent reason for remaining that way."

"BUT IT IS MADNESS, Savigny! A brilliant doctor like you, a celebrity by now . . . now that the doors of the Academy are about to be thrown open before you . . . You know very well, that study of yours on the effects of hunger and thirst . . . well, even though I deem it more romantic than scientific . . ."

"My Lord Baron . . ."

". . . however, it has made a great impression on my colleagues and I am happy for you, the Academy bows before your charm and . . . also before your . . . painful experiences . . . I can understand it . . . but what I cannot understand is why you have got it into your head, now of all times, to go and hide in some godforsaken hole in the provinces to play, hear ye hear ye, *the country doctor*, am I right?"

"Yes, My Lord Baron."

"Oh, congratulations . . . there is no doctor in this city who would not want, but what am I saying, who *would not love to have* your name and your brilliant future, and what do you decide to do? To go off and practice in some village . . . and what kind of village would it be, come to that?"

"In the country."

"I have understood that much, but where?"

"Far away."

"Must I deduce that one may not know where?"

"That is my wish, my lord Baron."

"Absurd. You are pitiful, Savigny, you are worthless, unreasonable, execrable. I can find no plausible justification for this unpardonable attitude of yours and . . . and . . . I cannot think other than this: you are mad, sir!"

"It's the other way around: I don't wish to become so, my lord Baron."

"Look . . . that's Charbonne . . . do you see it down there?"

"Yes."

"It's a fine little town. You will like it there."

"Yes."

"Sit yourself up, Doctor . . . that's it. Hold this a moment for me, that's it . . . You have been raving all night long, you must do something . . ."

"I told you that there was no need to stay on here, Marie."

"What are you doing? . . . you are not thinking of getting up . . ."

"Of course I am going to get up . . ."

"But you cannot . . ."

"Marie, I'm the doctor."

"Yes, but you did not see yourself last night . . . you were really ill, you seemed a madman, you were talking to ghosts, and you were shouting . . ."

"Shouting?"

"You were angry with the sea."

"Ohhh, again?"

"You have some bad memories, Doctor. And bad memories spoil life."

"It's bad life, Marie, that spoils memories."

"But you are not bad."

"I did some things, down there. And they were horrendous things."

"Why?"

"They were horrendous. No one could forgive them. No one has forgiven me for them."

"You mustn't think about it anymore . . ."

"And what is even more horrendous is this: I know that, today, if I were to go back down there, I would do the same things again."

"Stop it, Doctor . . ."

"I know I would do the same things again, the exact same things. Isn't that monstrous?"

"Doctor, I beg you . . ."

"Isn't that monstrous?"

"THE NIGHTS ARE getting colder again . . ."

"Yes."

"I'd like to take you home, Doctor, but I don't want to leave my wife alone . . ."

"No, don't put yourself out."

"However . . . I want you to know that conversing with you is a great pleasure for me."

"For me, too."

"You know, when you came here, a year ago, they said you were . . ."

"A haughty and arrogant doctor from the capital . . ."

"Yes, more or less. The folk here are suspicious. Every so often they get hold of strange ideas."

"Do you know what they said to me, about you?"

"That I was rich."

"Yes."

"And taciturn."

"Yes. But also that you were a good man."

"It's as I told you: the folk here get hold of some strange ideas."

"It's curious. To think of staying here. For a man like me . . . an arrogant doctor from the capital . . . to think of growing old here."

"It seems to me that you are still a little too young to start thinking about where to grow old, don't you agree?"

"Perhaps you are right. But here is so far away from everything . . . I wonder if anything will ever manage to take me away again."

"Don't think about it. If it happens, it will be something good. And if not, this town will be glad to keep you for itself."

"It's an honor to hear it said by the mayor in person . . ."

"Oh, don't remind me, I beg you . . ."

"I must really go now."

"Yes. But come back, when you wish. I should like that. And my wife too would be most happy."

"Count on it."

"Good night, then, Dr. Savigny."

"Good night, Monsieur Deverià."

CHAPTER 7

Adams

H E STAYED AWAKE for hours, after sunset. The last innocent time of a whole life.

Then he left his room and walked silently along the corridor until he came to a stop in front of the last door. There were no keys in the Almayer Inn.

One hand resting on the doorknob, the other holding a small candleholder. Moments like needles. The door opened without a sound. Silence and darkness, inside the room.

He went in, put the candleholder down on the writing desk, and closed the door behind him. The click of the lock made a sharp sound in the night: in the half-light, between the sheets, something moved.

He went up to the bed and said, "It's over, Savigny."

A phrase like a saber cut. Savigny shot upright in bed, lashed by a thrill of terror. Questing in the tepid light of those few candles, his eyes caught the glitter of a knifeblade and, motionless, the face of a man whom he had been trying for years to forget.

"Thomas . . ."

Ann Deverià looked at him, bewildered. She propped herself up on one arm, cast a glance around the room, she did not understand, she sought again the face of her lover, she slid close to him.

"What is happening, André?"

He kept on staring, terrified, straight ahead.

"Thomas, stop, you're mad . . ."

But he did not stop. He came right up to the bed, raised his knife, and brought it down again violently, once. Twice, three times. The covers were soaked with blood.

Ann Deverià did not even have the time to cry out. Stupefied, she stared at the dark tide that was spreading over her and she felt life slipping away from that open body of hers, so fast that it did not even leave her the time for a thought. She slumped backward, with staring eyes that could no longer see anything.

Savigny was trembling. There was blood everywhere. And an absurd silence. It was at rest, the Almayer Inn. Motionless.

"Get up, Savigny. And take her in your arms."

Thomas's voice resounded with an inexorable tranquillity. It was not over yet, no.

Savigny moved as if in a trance. He got up, picked up Ann Deverià's body, and, holding it in his arms, he let himself be dragged out of the room. He could not manage to say a word. He could see nothing anymore, nor could he manage to think. He was trembling, that's all.

Strange little procession. The beautiful body of a woman borne in procession. A dead burden of blood in the arms of a man who dragged himself along trembling, followed by an impassive shadow with a knife clutched in his fist. They crossed the inn like that, until they were out onto the beach. One step after another, in the sand, until they reached the seashore. A wake of blood behind them. A little moonlight upon them.

"Don't stop, Savigny."

Swaying, he forced his feet into the water. He could feel that knife pressed against his back, and, in his arms, a weight that was becoming enormous. Like a puppet he dragged himself on for a few yards. That voice stopped him.

"Listen to it, Savigny. It's the sound of the sea. May this sound and that weight in your arms follow you for the rest of your life."

He said it slowly, without emotion and with a hint of tiredness. Then he let the knife fall into the water, turned around and headed back to the beach. He crossed it, following those dark blotches, congealed in the sand. He was walking slowly, with no more thoughts and no more story.

Nailed to the threshold of the sea, with the waves foaming between his legs, Savigny stood motionless, incapable of any gesture. He was trembling. And he was weeping. A puppet, a child, a wreck. He was dripping blood and tears: the wax of a candle that no one would ever be able to extinguish.

ADAMS WAS HANGED, in the town square of St. Amand, at dawn on the last day of April. It was raining heavily, but many had come out to enjoy the spectacle. They buried him that same day. No one knows where.

CHAPTER 8

The Seventh Room

T HE DOOR OPENED, and a man came out of the
seventh room. One step beyond the threshold, he
stopped and looked around. The inn seemed deserted.
Not a sound, not a voice, nothing. The sun was coming in
through the little windows in the corridor, cutting the dim
light and projecting small trailers for a clear and bright morning on the wall.

Inside the room, everything had been put in order in a willing but hasty fashion. A full suitcase, still open, on the bed.
Sheets of paper in piles on the desk, pens, books, a lamp,
switched off. Two plates and a glass on the windowsill. Dirty
but ordered. On the floor, a corner of the carpet formed a
large dog-ear, as if someone had left a sign in order to find the

place again one day. On the armchair was a large blanket, folded roughly. Two pictures could be seen on a wall. Identical.

Leaving the door open behind him, the man went along the corridor and went down the stairs, singing a cryptic little refrain softly to himself, and he stopped at the reception desk—if we want to call it that. Dira was not there. There was the usual register, open on the book rest. The man began reading, tucking his shirt into his trousers as he did so. Funny names. He looked around again. The Almayer was decidedly the most deserted inn in the history of deserted inns. He entered the large lounge, walked around the tables for a bit, sniffed at a bunch of flowers growing old in a horrendous crystal vase, went up to the glass door, and opened it.

That air. And the light.

He had to half close his eyes, it was so strong, and pull his jacket closer around him against all that wind from the north.

Ahead, the whole beach. He set his feet on the sand. He was looking at them as if in that moment they had returned from a long journey. He seemed genuinely amazed that they were there once more. He looked up again, and his face bore that expression which people have, every so often, when the mind is empty, emptied, happy. Such moments are strange. Without knowing why, you could commit any act of foolishness. He committed a very simple one. He began to run, but he ran like mad, at breakneck speed, tripping and getting up again, without ever stopping, running as fast as he could, as if he had the devil at his heels, but there was no one at his heels, no, it was he who was running and that was it, he alone, along that deserted beach, with his eyes staring and his heart in his

232

mouth, it was the sort of thing that, had you seen him, you would have said, "He won't stop."

Seated on his usual windowsill, his legs dangling out into empty space, Dood took his eyes off the sea, turned toward the beach, and saw him.

He was running brilliantly, no argument about that.

Dood smiled.

"He has finished."

Beside him was Ditz, the one who invented dreams and then made you a present of them.

"Either he's gone mad, or he has finished."

IN THE AFTERNOON, everybody was on the shore, throwing flat stones to make them skip, and throwing round stones to hear them splash. They were all there: Dood, who had come down from his windowsill specially; Ditz, the one with the dreams; Dol, who had seen so many ships for Plasson. There was Dira. And there was the astonishingly beautiful little girl that slept in bed with Ann Deverià, and who knows what her name was. All there, throwing stones in the water and listening to that man who had come out of the seventh room. He was talking very slowly.

"You have to imagine two people who love each other . . . who love each other. And he must go away. He is a sailor. He is leaving for a long journey, at sea. And so she embroiders a silk handkerchief with her own hands . . . she embroiders her name upon it."

"June."

"June. She embroiders it in red thread. And she thinks: he will always carry it with him, and this will protect him from dangers, from storms, from diseases . . ."

"From big fish."

". . . from big fish . . ."

"From the bananafish."

". . . from everything. She is convinced of it. But she doesn't give it to him straightaway, no. First she takes it to her village church and says to the priest, 'You must bless it.' And so the priest puts it down there, in front of him, he bends over a little, and with a finger he draws a cross above it. He says something in a strange language, and with a finger he draws a cross above it. Can you manage to imagine it? A tiny little gesture. The handkerchief, that finger, the priest's words, her eyes, smiling. Is that all perfectly clear to you?"

"Yes."

"Right, then, now imagine this. A ship. Big. About to set sail."

"The ship of the sailor you mentioned before?"

"No. Another ship. But she, too, is about to set sail. They have cleaned her very well all over. She is floating on the water in the harbor. And before her, miles and miles of sea are waiting, the sea with its immense strength, the mad sea, perhaps it will be kind, but perhaps it will crush her in its hands and swallow her, who knows? No one talks about it, but everyone knows how strong the sea is. And then a little man, dressed in black, boards that ship. All the sailors are on deck, with their families, the women, the children, all there, standing in silence. The little man walks about the ship, murmuring something

234

under his breath. He goes as far as the prow, then he turns back, walking slowly among the cordage, the folded sails, the casks, the nets. He is still murmuring strange things to himself, and there is no corner of the ship that he does not visit. In the end he stops, in the middle of the bridge. And he kneels. He lowers his head and continues murmuring in that strange tongue of his, it seems as if he is talking to the ship, that he is telling her something. Then suddenly he is silent, and with one hand, slowly, he draws the sign of the cross above those wooden planks. The sign of the cross. And then everyone turns toward the sea, and they have the look of those who have won, because they know that that ship will return, she is a blessed ship, she will challenge the sea and win, nothing can harm her anymore. She is a blessed ship."

They had even stopped throwing stones in the water. By that time they were motionless, listening. Sitting on the sand, all five of them, and around, for miles, no one.

"Have you got it clear?"

"Yes."

"Can all of you see it, really well?"

"Yes."

"Then listen carefully. Because here it gets difficult. An old man. With white, white skin, lean hands; he walks with difficulty, slowly. He is going up the main street of a town. Behind him, hundreds and hundreds of people, all the people of the town, filing past and singing, they are wearing their best clothes, no one is absent. The old man keeps on walking, and he seems alone, completely alone. He arrives at the last houses in the town, but he does not stop. He is so old that his hands shake, and his head too, a bit. But he looks straight ahead, calm, and he does not stop even at the beginning of the beach. He slips between the boats hauled up above the waterline, with that unsteady gait of his that makes it seem as if he will fall at any moment, but he never does. Behind him, all the others, a few yards behind, but still there. Hundreds and hundreds of people. The old man walks on the sand, and it's even more complicated, but it doesn't matter, he will not stop, and since he does not stop, in the end he comes to the sea. The sea. The people stop singing, they stop a few steps away from the shore. Now he seems even more alone, the old man, while he places one foot in front of the other, so slowly, and walks into the sea, a man alone, in the sea. A few steps, until the water reaches his knees. His clothes, soaked through, cling to him and those terribly skinny legs, skin and bone. The wave slips back and forth and he is so slight that you think it will carry him off. But it doesn't, he stays there, as if planted in the water, his eyes staring straight ahead of him. His eyes looking straight into those of the sea. Silence. All around, nothing stirs. The people hold their breath. A spell.

Then
the old man
lowers
his eyes,
immerses
a hand
in the water,
and
slowly

236

draws

the sign

of the cross.

Slowly. *He says a prayer for the sea.*

And it is an enormous thing, you must try to imagine it, a weak old man, a trifling gesture, and suddenly the immense sea is shaken, the entire sea, as far as the farthest horizon, trembles, shakes, dissolves, as into its veins slips the honey of a blessing that enthralls every wave, and all the ships in the world, the squalls, the deepest abysses, the darkest waters, the men and the animals, those who are dying, those who are afraid, those who are watching, bewitched, terrified, moved, happy, transported, when suddenly, for an instant, the immense sea bows its head, and it is an enigma no longer, it is an enemy no longer, it is no longer silence but a brother, and a docile womb, and a spectacle for men saved. An old man's hand. A sign, in the water. You look at the sea and it doesn't frighten you anymore. The end.

Silence.

What a story, thought Dood. Dira turned to look at the sea. What a story. The beautiful little girl sniffed. Can it be true? thought Ditz.

The man stayed seated, on the sand, and said nothing.

Dol looked him in the eye.

"Is it a true story?"

"It was."

"And it isn't anymore?"

"No."

"Why?"

237

"You cannot say a prayer for the sea anymore."

"But that old man could."

"That old man was old and had something inside that doesn't exist anymore."

"Magic?"

"Something of the sort. A beautiful magic."

"And where did it go?"

"It vanished."

They couldn't believe that it had really disappeared into nothingness.

"Do you swear it?"

"I swear it."

It had really disappeared.

The man got up. In the distance you could see the Almayer Inn, almost transparent in that light laved by the north wind. The sun seemed to have stopped in the clearer half of the sky. And Dira said, "You came here to say a prayer for the sea, didn't you?"

The man looked at her, took a few steps, came up close to her, bent over, and smiled.

"No."

"So what were you doing in that room?"

"Although you cannot say a prayer for the sea anymore, perhaps you can still *say* the sea."

Say the sea. Say the sea. *Say the sea.* So that not all that was in the gesture of that old man is lost, so that perhaps a drop of that magic may wander through time, and something might find it, and save it before it disappears forever. Say the sea. Because it's what we have left. Because faced by the sea, we without crosses, without old men, without magic, we must still have a weapon, something, so as not to die in silence, that's all.

"*Say* the sea."

"Yes."

"And you were in there all that time, saying the sea."

"Yes."

"But to whom?"

"It doesn't matter to whom. The important thing is trying to say it. Someone will listen."

They had thought he was a bit odd. But not in that way. In a simpler way.

"And you need all those sheets of paper to say it?"

Dood had had to lug that big bag full of paper all the way down the stairs. It had stuck in his craw, that business.

"Well, no. If someone were really able, all he would need is a few words . . . Perhaps he would begin with lots of pages, but then, little by little, he would find the right words, those that say in one go what all the others do, and from a thousand pages he would get down to a hundred, and then to ten, and then he would leave them there, to wait, until the excess words slipped off the pages, and then all you would have to do would be to collect the remaining words, and compress them into fewer words, ten, five, so few that by dint of looking at them from close up, and listening to them, in the end you would be left with one, only one. And if you say it, you say the sea."

"Only one?"

"Yes."

"Which one?"

"Who knows?"

"Any word?"

"A word."

"But even a word like *potato*?"

"Yes. Or *help!*, or *etcetera*, you cannot know until you find it."

As he talked he was looking around in the sand, the man from the seventh room. He was looking for a stone.

"Excuse me . . ." said Dood.

"What?"

"Can't you use *sea*?"

"No you can't use *sea*."

He had got up. He had found the stone.

"Then it's impossible. It's an impossibility."

"Who knows what's impossible?"

He went up to the sea and threw the stone far away into the water. It was a round stone.

"Splash," said Dol, who was a connoisseur.

But the stone began to skip, on the surface of the water, once, twice, three times, it just kept going, skipping wonderfully, farther and farther, it was skipping out to sea, as if they had liberated it. It seemed as if it never wanted to stop again. And it never stopped again.

THE MAN LEFT the inn the following morning. There was a strange sky, one of those that scud along fast, in a hurry to get home. The north wind was blowing, strongly but soundlessly. The man liked walking. He took his suitcase and his bag full of paper and set off along the road that flanked the coast. He walked quickly, without ever looking back. And so he did not see the Almayer Inn detach itself from the ground and break up airily into a thousand pieces, which looked like sails and floated up in the air, going up and down, *flying*, and they took everything with them, far away, that sea and that land, and the words and the stories, everything, who knows where, no one knows, perhaps one day someone will be so tired that he will find out.

TURN THE PAGE TO FIND AN EXTRACT
FROM THE INTERNATIONAL BESTSELLER AND FILM

SILK

Translated from the Italian by Ann Goldstein

£7.99

ISBN 978 1 84195 835 4

France, 1861. When an epidemic threatens the silk trade, a young silk-
worm breeder has to travel to distant Japan to smuggle out healthy
worms. His attention is arrested by a local baron's concubine, a girl who
does not have oriental eyes. Although they are unable to exchange a
word, love blossoms between them.

'A heart-breaking love story told in the form of a classic fable . . .
A literary gem of bewitching power.' *Sunday Times*

'One of the most astonishing and moving novels I have read.' *Daily Telegraph*

FOR MORE BY ALESSANDRO BARICCO, READ ON...

A rice-paper panel slid open, and Hervé Joncour entered. Hara Kei was sitting cross-legged, on the floor, in the furthest corner of the room. He had on a dark tunic, and wore no jewels. The only visible sign of his power was a woman lying beside him, unmoving, her head resting on his lap, eyes closed, arms hidden under a loose red robe that spread around her, like a flame, on the ash-coloured mat. Slowly he ran one hand through her hair: he seemed to be caressing the coat of a precious, sleeping animal.

Hervé Joncour crossed the room, waited for a sign from his host, and sat down opposite him. A servant arrived, imperceptibly, and placed before them two cups of tea. Then he vanished. Hara Kei began to speak, in his own language, in a singsong voice that melted into a sort of irritating artificial falsetto. Hervé Joncour listened. He kept his eyes fixed on those of Hara Kei and only for an instant, almost without realising it, lowered them to the face of the woman.

It was the face of a girl.

He raised them again.

Hara Kei paused, picked up one of the cups of tea, brought it to his lips, let some moments pass and said

'Try to tell me who you are.'

He said it in French, drawing out the vowels, in a hoarse voice but true.

***

To the most invincible man in Japan, the master of all that the world might take away from that island, Hervé Joncour tried to explain who he was. He did it in his own language, speaking slowly, without knowing precisely if Hara Kei was able to understand. Instinctively he rejected prudence, reporting simply, without inventions and without omissions, everything that was true. He set forth small details and crucial events in the same tone, and with barely visible gestures, imitating the hypnotic pace, melancholy and neutral, of a catalogue of objects rescued from a fire. Hara Kei listened, and not a shadow of an expression discomposed the features of his face. He kept his eyes fixed on Hervé Joncour's lips, as if they were the last lines of a farewell letter. The room was so silent and still that what happened unexpectedly seemed a huge event and yet was nothing.

Suddenly,

without moving at all,

that girl

opened her eyes.

Hervé Joncour did not pause but instinctively lowered his gaze to her, and what he saw, without pausing, was that those eyes *did not have an Oriental shape*, and that they were fixed, *with a disconcerting intensity*, on him: as if from the start, from under the eyelids, they had done nothing else. Hervé Joncour turned his gaze elsewhere, as naturally as he could, trying to continue his story with no perceptible difference in his voice. He stopped only when his eyes fell on the cup of tea, placed on the floor, in front of him. He took it in one hand, brought it to his lips, and drank slowly. He began to speak again as he set it down in front of him.

***

France, the ocean voyages, the scent of the mulberry trees in Lavilledieu, the steam trains, Hélène's voice. Hervé Joncour continued to recount his story, as he had never in his life done. The girl continued to stare at him, with a violence that wrenched from every word the obligation to be memorable. The room seemed to have slipped into an irreversible stillness when suddenly, and in utter silence, she stuck one hand outside her robe and slid it along the mat in front of her. Hervé Joncour saw that pale spot reach the edge of his field of vision, saw it touch Hara Kei's cup of tea and then, absurdly, continue to slide until, without hesitation, it grasped the other cup, which was inexorably the cup he had drunk from, raised it lightly, and carried it away. Not for an instant had Hara Kei stopped staring expressionlessly at Hervé Joncour's lips.

The girl lifted her head slightly.

For the first time she took her eyes off Hervé Joncour and rested them on the cup.

Slowly, she rotated it until she had her lips at the exact point where he had drunk.

Half-closing her eyes, she took a sip of tea.

She removed the cup from her lips.

She slid it back to where she had picked it up.

Her hand vanished under her robe.

She rested her head again on Hara Kei's lap.

Eyes open, fixed on those of Hervé Joncour.

***

Hervé Joncour spoke again at length. He stopped only when Hara Kei took his eyes off him and nodded his head slightly.

Silence.

In French, drawing out the vowels, in a hoarse voice but true, Hara Kei said

'If you are willing, I would like to see you return.'

For the first time he smiled.

'The eggs you have with you are fish eggs, worth little more than nothing.'

Hervé Joncour lowered his gaze. There was his cup of tea, in front of him. He picked it up and began to revolve it, and to observe it, as if he were searching for something on the painted line of the rim. When he found what he was looking for, he placed his lips there and drank. Then he put the cup down in front of him and said

'I know.'

Hara Kei laughed in amusement.

'Is that why you paid in false gold?'

'I paid for what I bought.'

Hara Kei became serious again.

'When you leave here you will have what you want.'

'When I leave this island, alive, you will receive the gold that is due you. You have my word.'

Hervé Joncour did not expect an answer. He rose, took a few steps backward, and bowed.

The last thing he saw, before he left, was her eyes, staring into his, perfectly mute.

WITHOUT BLOOD

ALESSANDRO BARICCO

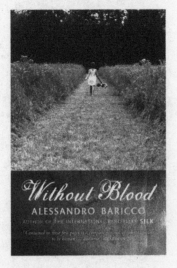

Beginning with a shocking act of violence – the assassination of a man
and his family – *Without Blood* is a haunting book about damage, longing
and forgiveness. Decades after the attack, sole survivor Nina hunts down
the last of her family's murderers, the man who also allowed her to
escape with her life. Ann Goldstein's superb translation has captured
Baricco's effortless prose to give us a gem of a novel that has already
delighted hundreds of thousands across Europe.

'Contained in these pages is a complete portrait of what it means to be
human . . . awesome.' *Guardian*

£7.99

ISBN 978 1 84195 574 2

www.canongate.tv

AN ILIAD
ALESSANDRO BARICCO

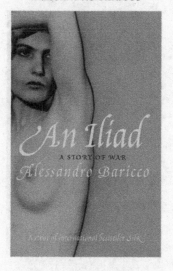

In this bravura piece of storytelling, Alessandro Baricco recreates the
siege of Troy through the eyes and voices of each of the twenty-one
major Homeric characters in turn. Through their personal experiences,
we witness the unforgettable war first told of thousands of years ago.
Baricco has transformed Homer's masterwork into a vivid retelling
resounding with love, jealousy and the eternal energy of conflict.

'A swift, stylish, summer-reading version of the great epic.'
San Francisco Chronicle

£8.99

ISBN 978 1 84767 103 5

www.canongate.tv